PRAISE THE SOULS OF HER FEET

*"*The Souls of Her Feet *was a joy to read. I felt young again, and excited about love after reading. It inspired me to create a clown show based on the book so enough said there!"*

—Tristan Cunningham, actor & clown

"A decidedly different approach to the Cinderella story—sit back, relax and put on your best pair of dancing shoes—even if they are a size twelve."

—Elaine Webster, California Writers Club

"Get me a ticket to Broadway so I can be the first to see this in the theater! Kristen Caven has magically combined all of the elements of being a teenage girl on the cusp of discovering and living her strengths with the true meaning of internal and external beauty. Her contemporary Cinderella renews the universal message to girls about the ability to overcome life's obstacles and how to make the most of the fabulous power of Different. Bravo."

—Sheryl Bize-Boutte, author of *A Dollar Five*

*"*The Souls of Her Feet *is a clever, fun read loaded with vintage shoe detail and a bit of shoe philosophy, to boot!"*

—Moya Stone, fashion blogger, *Overdressed for Life*

"This was such a fun read! I just loved it! Kristen has the skilled hand that it takes to retell a fairy tale without coming off clichéd or overly sentimental. Strong voice, great characters, and upbeat pacing drive this story through to the very end. I identified so much with the cleaning-as-therapy that Ashley begins. I dearly, dearly love Harry! But my absolute favorite part is the 'glass slipper.'"

—JM Randolph, blogger, *The Accidental Stepmom*

I found myself reading and reading and reading ("just one more chapter then I'll stop... ok, just one more... ok now REALLY just one more...")

—Pam Consear, All Hands Art

"I loved the psychological nuances. Clearly she knows about stepfamilies."

—Ani Liggett, author, *Endings. Beginnings...*

"I love this book! I've read it over and over again. The Souls of Her Feet *is the story of a verbally- and emotionally-abused teenager, discovering and creating her authentic Self. One weekend, a special person from her past arrives, and suddenly her painful teen years start to blossom into a womanhood full of promise and joy. The writing throughout is packed with humor, imagination and great quotes. I highly recommend this to anyone who has ever struggled with body issues, self-esteem, deceased parents or a dysfunctional family, no matter who you are or what your circumstances."*

—Dr. Louise Hart, psychologist & author of *The Winning Family, On the Wings of Self-Esteem, The Bullying Antidote*

"At last, a Cinderella story for people who like shoes but are tired of all that magick-y, princess-y shit."

—Comment at a *Souls of Her Feet SHOE SALON*

"I would give this book a five if it didn't have swearing words. It had a lot of detail and made me cry."

—Nicole, 9, Amazon Reviewer

THE SOULS OF HER FEET

a novel

By Kristen Caven

The Souls of Her Feet

Book One of *The Fairytale Reality Project*

Based on the musical, *The Souls of Her Feet*, part one of *Shoes, a Mirror, and a Big, Pink Rose* © 2001 by Kristen Caven.

This book is a work of fiction straight from the author's imagination. Any resemblances to historical events, real people or places, or other fictitious works are purely coincidental.

Uplift Press | www.upliftpress.com

Fourth paperback edition 2019

ISBN-10: 1-950282-49-X

ISBN-13: 978-1-950282-49-4

Contact the author for speaking events or about the musical.

Cover Model: Charlotte Hutcheson Wilcox

Cover Photo: Ann Hutcheson Wilcox

Author Photo: Jennifer Flynn Israel

Book Design & Illustrations: Kristen Caven

Text is set in Georgia with asides in Edwardian Script

is a concept sketch by Steven Arpad, circa 1939, public domain.

FOREWORD

Once upon a time, there were a writer and a composer who were in love. Not with each other—though they liked each other a lot—but with the way you can move hearts with music and stories.

The writer was fascinated by the way certain folk tales are told and retold and come alive again, generation after generation. (Especially once Disney got hold of them.) She imagined this is because sometimes, for a moment, our lives as regular people feel like fairytales, and resonate with greater meaning.

But even though we all love fairytales, wouldn't it really kind of suck to live in one? She and the composer thought up a contest to find young people who had had real-life experiences that seemed like fairytales. They started The Fairytale Reality Project.

Just like the shoe in the Cinderella story, it was hard to find one, among the many submissions, that was "a perfect fit."

But then one day, there came a letter.

My Dear Creatives,

All of my freshmen students are twittering—in the Twentieth Century sense of the word at least; perhaps in the other way as well—about your contest. Several of them have entered it with clever and creatively embroidered versions of their lives. Still, I admire your pursuit, and respect it, as it mirrors my own, less formal, survey of lives with fairytale parallels.

I am a professor of Mythological Studies at Castleton College, and, as well as building cultural literacy in the fertile minds of eighteen-year-olds, I also try to teach my students to look at their lives with a little perspective, seeing the stories we study as metaphor. I ask them, "What is your personal fairytale life?" Oh, they have wonderful imaginations. Everyone can find some story, somewhere, with connection to their own, for this is why we human folks have stories. But the ones who actually live out a big myth are rare, and this is a good thing, for it disturbs the soul and can warp the mind. And furthermore, some of the stories we love most deal with sorrows we hope never to encounter (dead mothers, absent fathers, injustice, people trying to kill them); and it is best when these things are rare. But pain is a game life plays with us, is it not?

In the first fall semester of the millennium, however, I experienced a coincidence that has borne out into the most unusual story. In short: I believe I found what you are looking for! There were three girls in my Folktales 101 class who had all lost their mothers. Two of them, Ashley St. Helens and Nevada LeBlanc, had been friends from high school; they quickly bonded with the third, Linda Loveland. Special people, all of them; (teachers find, over the years, that the good ones travel in groups;) I have maintained a friendship with each of them over the years, and their unfolding lives have amazed me. They will amaze you.

Particularly Ashely St. Helens. When this young lady first walked into my classroom, I could see at once that she was a notch more confident, self-assured, and joyful than your average freshman co-ed, with a personal energy that flowed from a deep well-spring. (A nice sense of humor; in her First Day Interview, I recall she mentioned a loathing of unicorns.) She was tall to begin with, but carried herself regally...and yet a little awkwardly, at the same time. 'As if,' was my first, surprising impression, 'she had only recently learned to stand up straight.' At first I had trouble identifying her, since the photographs in our original student file had come from their high-school application packet. I was trying to match up a flat-haired, blank-faced, sad, insecure thing, lost in an oversized sweatshirt, with the radiant being that strode into my classroom each day. And her clothes.

And her shoes! Ashley always looks expressively well put-together, creatively dressed, fun and elegant. Whence this transformation? Ashley was a mystery to me, and when I got to know her story. (And how could I have missed it? It was in all the local papers, but the answer to that is, of course, that I live in an ivory tower! But I digress.) I encouraged her to write her history, since writing our stories helps us discover the greater meaning in our lives. Over the years, I was fortunate to become her advisor, and for her senior project as an English Major, she developed it into a lovely read that I have urged her to send you.

I think it would make a wonderful musical. Who wouldn't love a song about shoes?

Conspiritorially,

Illegible Squiggle

Professor Mädchen März, Ph.D[i]*.*
Department Head, Folklore
Castleton College
Black Forest, MW 44883

TABLE OF CONTENTS

1 ONCE UPON A TIME

My first word was "Thanks." My first sentence, "Excuse me." My parents showed me how to be polite and well-spoken, to polish my best qualities, and to be kind to others...which I never realized until after they were both gone. As college students, they had been drawn to one another by mutual ideals of personal responsibility, community service, and human potential. My mother wore flowered frocks and a wide smile at all times, and brought an air of sweetness to her every endeavor. My father surrounded her, at times like a garden wall, at other times like a large and exuberant puppy.

Dad was absolutely dedicated to our family, and frequently begged my mom for more children. "But darling," she'd say, knowing she was playing a role, and that his playful begging was an act, since they both knew it wasn't in the cards, "we got it right the first time; we don't need any more kids." And so it was that I knew I was special, and therefore checked my small wishes for siblings before they could turn into actual longings. I was never lonely. Mom, the consummate housewife, taught me to sew, to cook, and so many ways to clean that it never felt like a chore. And I loved to read; reading was a big part of all of our lives, always the reward for when the work was done. Quiet evenings snuggled by the fire, Saturdays in the sun, it's no wonder I did well in school. Being kind, I always had friends, but never felt I needed them, since my family was my world.

When I got to middle school, though, life got more complicated, as life does for all of us when we reach a certain age and the innocence falls away. You start wondering about Santa Claus, and then you start wondering about everything else. I wondered why my father was so distractible, and why my mother was so passionate about keeping things just so. I never got a chance to answer these questions, since the fates had other plans for us all. I was in eighth grade Science class when I got called to the office with the news my mother was in the hospital. It sounds funny to say mom died in a tragic cleaning accident, but that's what happened, and it wasn't funny at all; it was the most horrible day of my life. When I studied Chemistry in college I came to understand what I didn't then: never, ever mix ammonia with chlorine bleach. And never, ever, ever let toilet cleaner near drain cleaner. Enough said.

In tenth grade, my dad got married to Sylvia, a nice lady from our church who was very kind and clear about how she wanted to take care of him (and after a few years of living alone with him, I was starting to realize how much he needed to be taken care of). I got two sisters my own age out of the deal. After living in an empty house with dad for a year, our life, at first, was like a slumber party that didn't end. Debra and Donna were empty-headed and light-hearted; their focus on fashion and teen-hunks was refreshing and cheered me up.

I wanted them to like me. But I was uncomfortable the way Sylvia would yell at them, build them up and tear them down, in a way I had never seen before; my parents never treated *anyone* like that. Sylvia would never raise her voice around dad, of course, and only little by little, around me. Then one day she yelled at me on the way out the door to school to "get my ass moving." It was weird that what I felt was a sense of relief at her harsh words and tone. I knew who she was now; I felt like, for the first time, she was treating me as one of her own. I still hoped that she could be a good mom to me, that we could someday, somehow, feel close. Well, I decided, if that's what it takes....

My father was clear from the start, that he intended to treat us all equally, and I was glad for him that his wish for more kids was finally coming true, even if it wasn't with mom. "I don't want to play my kid/your kids," he said to Sylvia, as they discussed their wedding over dinner one night; "they're all our kids." I admired his attitude, admired him, and Debra, Donna and I all grinned at each other. Sylvia nodded and seemed to agree with this idea—to his face. But over time it dawned on me what was really happening. Sylvia, when she wasn't yelling at Debra and

Donna, was caring for them, talking to them, helping them in all the ways a mother helps her kids. On the other hand, when Dad wasn't around, she never really talked to me much, except in that "move your ass" tone of voice.

Then one day he found the truth out—yes, one horrible, horrible day, the *other* most horrible day in my life.

The Terrible Saturday started out nice and sisterly. Debra, Donna, and I had finished our homework, and were playing a board game and talking about boys. Well, *they* were talking about boys. I was half-listening in, my mind focused on a final decision whether it was Professor Plum or Miss White in the "Confidential" file. The two of them were arguing over this boy, yes, this boy named *Jeff* (*sigh*), who had, coincidentally, been my sweetheart in second grade, but with whom I wasn't that close anymore (not being close to anyone). It was fun to hear them talk about him, since I felt like I knew him so well (ha ha) and in my heart, I could tell there was still a sweetness between us, even while he was surrounded by his popular friends, or playing basketball, or helping a group of special needs kids cross the street.

"He's dating that beautiful cheerleader with the black hair," said Donna.

"No, he's not, I heard him say he was on his own. They're just friends," said Debra.

"You don't talk to him!"

"No, but I sit behind him in Psychology."

"That's why you're probably going to flunk that class."

And so forth.

Suddenly Sylvia was standing there, just out of her bath, wearing her fluffy robe, her hair in a yellow terrycloth turban... and holding a stack of lavender bath towels.

"You folded these, didn't you?" she asked me. I nodded, smiling, glad she had noticed. She had asked for help with the laundry, and I was glad to do it. I was used to working. Well, the next thing she did was drop the stack on the board, scattering our game across the polished tabletop. "Didn't your mother teach you anything? What is this?" She picked up the top towel and stared at it, then shook it in my face. "The edges are showing!" She snapped the towel open and laid it flat across the mess. "You fold towels in thirds. Pay attention, for once." She turned first one long edge in, then another, her movements intense with efficiency... and some weird rage I did not understand. Then she brought the folded ends over, one at a time, until the towel was a submissive package of gentle, well-behaved, and definitely humbled corners.

Debra and Donna had changed in her presence, from carefree companions to stiff and snooty judges, rolling their eyes, shaking their heads. Sylvia shoved the pile of towels at me and left the room with her girls. I sat there, stunned, kind of just trying to catch my breath, her question ringing in my ears: *Didn't your mother teach you anything?*

I bit my tongue, but I thought. *Didn't yours?*

At dinner that night the three of them chatted away with my dad, as if nothing unusual had happened, but I kept fighting back tears, trying to act normal, trying to *feel* normal, but inside, I was twisted up by what she'd said and how she'd talked to me. After dinner, Sylvia swept my dad away from the table to show him carpet samples for her redecorating plans, so I never got to talk to him. The Girls went off to talk on the phone, and I sat there at the table, surrounded by dirty dishes, feeling empty and alone, listening to the grandfather clock in the hall chime the half hour, then quarter of, then the hour of seven. Finally I decided to clean up. After all, it was my kitchen, too. And when I cleaned it, I could sometimes put things back where they belonged—back where they used to be.

When Sylvia came back to the kitchen, I had just started the dishwasher and was wiping the counter. She didn't say thanks or anything. Just, "Ugh, I sure don't want to see those pots and pans in the morning!"

That was too much. I remembered the tender moment after she had yelled at me the first time—but this was different. I squeezed the sponge in the sink, past the point where there was any water left, was hyper-aware of how my shoulders were positioned. I couldn't think of what to say, but something had to be said. I forced myself to ask, "Do you treat your daughters this way?" I mean, she did treat them pretty bad, but she never left the *cleaning* to them.

She could have said, "What do you mean?" We could have had a conversation, like people do, clearing the air. But Sylvia continued to take two wineglasses out of the cabinet. "Well," she shrugged, releasing me from any pretense, "I guess you're not my daughter."

Later, when I told my college pal Linda about Sylvia, she said Sylvia's icy manner was her way of masking her own buried pain, created by parents who never gave her the love she needed. Okay, I get that now, but at that moment I only felt confused at the wave of contempt that washed over me. Her blatant statement of rejection was completely unlike anything I'd ever experienced before. I stepped back at the force of it, feeling my breath escape me like when I fell off the monkey bars in second grade. And when I stepped back, I could see my dad's shadow blocking the door to the hallway. He had heard us speaking. I saw his face go white. Sylvia turned and saw him, looking stricken for a moment, caught in the act. Then she steeled herself, narrowed her eyes, waiting for a challenge. She didn't get one—my dad just stood there with a pained look on his face—so she gave one.

"Well, she's not!" Sylvia spat. "She's inattentive, reclusive, holier-than-thou, and defiant. You heard her tone." My mind reeled... was I really all those things? Inattentive, yeah, to some things, but on the other hand I had about a hundred more things to pay attention to than

Debra and Donna… like my studies, my volunteer work, my college applications, my sewing projects (many of which were for them), and my reading—I was working my way through my mother's book collection. "Whenever I say anything to her," Sylvia's voice went up a few notches, "I can tell she's just trying to imagine what her own mother would have said." Well, that part was actually true.

We both stared at my father's face, his very pale and slightly sweaty face, hoping he would say something that would support each of our points of view. I really needed him to stick up for me, to say something sweet, to tell her what a genuinely good person I was, how hard I tried to do the right thing, how I wasn't used to this sort of treatment and furthermore, I deserved better. I wanted him to say how Sylvia was the grown-up, and needed to take some responsibility for her part.

My dad's eyes unfocused just a little bit. He opened his mouth as if to say something, but no sound came out. He turned, instead, into the bathroom off the hallway, and threw up.

Then he passed out on the floor.

THE VIRTUE OF RAGS

After the funeral, I started hanging out in the attic where my mom's book collection had been banished to cardboard boxes (their shelves below long since appropriated for pictures of our new blended family, women's magazines, and kitschy knick-knacks). A serenity came over me each time I entered that peaked room, greeted by grandma's clothing dummy and grandpa's hatrack. Everything in the room was old, and therefore uninteresting to Donna and Debra, so I had my peace. Wood paneling ran up the slanted ceiling and the corners of the door were even carved off to fit the angles. A dormer window over the front driveway let in some nice afternoon sunlight.

I stacked an old mattress on top of the book boxes and would study in the afternoons, sometimes dozing off and not being missed by the others until morning; soon it became home base, and a perfect place to ride out my grief. I spent many hours just holding still. I'd find myself reading a paragraph over and over again, then let my eyes unfocus a bit, then find myself watching the dust motes float in a sunbeam, and wonder at them: *Are there dust motes in the shadows, too? Am I breathing dust motes? What are they made of? Are they all little worlds like in Horton Hears a Who?* These reveries would come upon me often that year, almost as if my organized mind went into idle so another part of me could grow. The Girls teased me about being ADD as kids still do. Sylvia criticized me for being 'spacey,' but she was right. In my mind I would hear my mother's voice, teasing me fondly for being a dreamer, but respecting the work of a woolgathering mind. (I talked to her a lot in the attic, where no one could judge me for being crazy.)

The rest of the house, which I passed through only to get food and use a bathroom, gradually became *theirs*. When the rare guest came over, Sylvia would host them in the slip-covered parlor just inside the front door, with all the other doors closed as if it were still the 1800s. Here's why: all of the other rooms were gradually being neglected to death. A shopping bag from Target would stay in the family room, not quite emptied. A spill on the stairs, when someone was bringing food to their room, would be left, and passing feet would grind Cheetos into the runners next to the piles of clothes that had sat there so long no one could remember if they were going up or down. Rubber bands from the newspapers sprang into corners, never to be retrieved, and the papers themselves would be left on a table after being read, open to the sale pages; or more often stacked up by the fireplace both unread and unburned. Hair scrunchies, clothing tags, toenail clippings, gum wrappers (and gum, itself), would be left behind without consciousness; no one ever had time to vacuum. Coffee rings and spilled food stayed on tabletops. Take-out containers, straws from sodas, lids from energy drink bottles were left on every horizontal surface. A former mocha latte with a layer of mold on it sat beside the television. And all of the casserole dishes and frozen dinner boxes that friends and neighbors brought by in sympathy just stacked up in the sink.

After a month or so, I couldn't stand it anymore; passing through the house on my way out the door would turn my stomach—and I never knew what I might step on. In a way, in a very twisted way, The Hills women did me a favor: their clutter eventually brought me out of my funk. One night I just started cleaning and it felt good. After that, when everyone went to bed at night I'd go attack a problem—the stairway, the kitchen, a bathroom. It was my house, my mother's house, and I didn't like to see it looking so awful.

Besides, all the yelling and whining was getting to me. "Where's my magazine?" "Has anyone seen my other leg warmer?" "I put my reading glasses right here and now they're gone." "I swear, this house is eating things!" "I swear, this house hates us!" "Mo-o-o-m!"

So, little by little, I took back the house.

When I told Linda this story—we were sitting on the lawn outside our dorms where we always had our best conversations—she was very impressed. "You know, dust and clutter create a very negative spiritual energy," she said. "There is a stickiness to it that attracts more dust and clutter, and this energy affects our minds, too. It's why the

Chinese start their new year with firecrackers, scaring that energy away, cleaning every corner of their house, getting new clothes and haircuts. It's good Feng Shui to have clean corners." There, I told myself, when she said this. There, I had been doing a spiritual service to myself, the Hills, and my parents all along. Without even knowing it. I had once read a book about a white witch that had this sentence in it: *when she cleaned up her house, she cleaned herself up inside, too.*[ii] Now I understood why my mother had been so dedicated to her household tasks.

I found some old clothes of mom's in a trunk—cute summer frocks and sweaters—and a box of sweatpants and t-shirts that my dad had collected from every college he'd visited at my age. The sweats became my uniforms when I cleaned. Eventually I started wearing them out of the house; there was never time to change. (At school, people started to think of me as very collegiate and sporty, my hair always in a ponytail.) The closeness of my dad made me feel so much better, and I was growing out of all of my old clothes, anyway.

I tore my worn-out nightgowns into flannel rags. Sylvia would screech in disgust when she saw me clean with them, diving for the chemical wipes that she trusted because they were advertised on TV. But one day when she came home I was carting a box of her chemical cleaners out the door, having replaced everything in the house with non-toxic substitutes. She had a fit but I held my ground. When she was done yelling, I just came right out and calmly reminded her how my mother had died.

That shut her up for a while.

I used to spend an hour or more in the laundry room each day, reading for AP English between tasks. The moist, tropical warmth of the dryer made it a cozy place. The loose ends of my hair would curl on their own, as if free for once to express themselves. One day I was sitting on the washer waiting for it to finish the spin cycle, lost in the dreamlike story and lulling motion of the machine. Just as it slowed to a stop, I read the last bittersweet sentence of Kafka's *Metamorphosis*. Everything was still for a moment, and as I pondered the similarities of Gregor Samsa's life with mine, far in the distance a curious thing happened: the phone rang.

In that house, I rarely heard the phone ring in the afternoon, since Debra or Donna were always talking on it and incoming calls would beep in their ears instead of out loud. A moment later, Donna burst into the room with said phone attached to the side of her head, blabbing away to one of her girlfriends about—as usual—clothes. (Let me try to record this faithfully; it was pretty amazing...)

"So did you see in the latest issue of TEEN PRINCESS they had those thigh-high stockings with the cross-stitched ribbing—no not those, those were cute too, but I don't like wide stripes, they make my legs look too fat—yes, and did

you see the SHOES she was wearing with them, oh my God, anyway, I'm all, aren't those adorable, just too too cute, and SO new they're just the thing, I have to have 'em, and I was like, trying to order them online but they declined my credit card because I've maxed it again and forgot I was waiting for Mother to get another mortgage, so I left 'em in my cart, since it may be awhile before I can get them—but I hope they're not like, totally out of style by the time I can complete the transaction, but anyway I have to Tweet and ask their circumference since my thighs are only sixteen inches and they might not even stay up."

I kid you not. One sentence.

Donna was generally so afraid of dirt, *and* of food, that there was never a chance she'd get any on her clothes, and since she would never exert herself, there was never a chance of B.O., either. Still, she'd bring me an outfit (or two, or five) every day to wash out the perfume, which she changed daily. In a typically brainless gesture, she dumped the pile right on the stack of laundry I had already folded.

Debra came in right behind her. Debra, who was a year older and about ten ounces heavier than Donna, always called her clothes by their proper name. "Ashley, here's my Spanx," she announced, "And my Juicy pants," with their name iced across the velour buttcheeks, "and... my cotton-candy Betsy Johnson cashmere shrug."

Debra was the big fan of designers, but Donna obsessed on the other labels, the little shiny white ones sewn in the seams. She rummaged through the pile she'd just tossed down, and located each care label, holding it up to my face to make sure I saw the little 'x' through the icon of the iron, or to have me decipher washing instructions printed in a European language.

"Here's *my* Nancy Ganz," she sung out, holding up a leopard-print bodyshaper and giving Debra's Spanx a superior look. Debra let out a *tsk!* and an exasperated breath as Donna fished for the label. "Hand-wash sep-a-rate-ly." She turned her great big brown eyes on me, checking for understanding. I held her gaze deliberately, pressing my lips together to keep the words in my head from coming out, and using all my willpower to avoid rolling my eyes at her sister. "These are power Lycra—see?" Donna pulled the waistband out two feet and let the elastic snap back to doll-size. "Steel-stretch!"

"Those are sure some super underpants," I nodded very slowly and appreciatively, a ritualistically ironic gesture I made several times a week. While I was nodding, I noticed my brain wondering why, at seventeen, Donna felt she needed tummy control. Nod, nod, nod. I said, "I'll make sure they smell dainty-fresh!"

Linda has helped me, since, to understand that Donna and Debra's body and food issues were inflamed by their perfectionist mother (the only one in the family who actually needed old-fashioned foundation garments to make her clothes work)... back then it baffled me why a size negative two would need such a thing. But just as I opened my mouth to say so, Sylvia, who entered a room chin-first (as if that made her taller somehow, and her cheekbones more aerodynamic), came through the swinging doors of that laundry room. Donna's babbling stopped cold. For a moment there, it seemed as if the fog clinging to the windows was frost.

Now it was Sylvia's turn to hand me a silky bundle. "I need this pressed, dear."

Quite baffled, I very emphatically did NOT point out the factor that, if there's a wrinkle in your girdle when it's hanging limp in your hands, it's not gonna be there the minute you stretch it across your bee-hind. Instead I said, "Sure, Sylvia," in a forcefully cheerful tone—my best way of maintaining my distance and avoiding any possibility of a fracas. (The night of many girdles, at least, later inspired me to write one of my best college essays.[iii])

I gathered Sylvia's creamy white Maidenform, Donna's animal-style Nancy Ganz, and Debra's flesh-toned Spanx in one hand. Then I reached for Debra's cotton-candy Betsy Johnson cashmere shrug, and said, with flight attendant's professional smile, "I'll do a load of hand wash delicates right now."

It was as if I'd just announced my intentions to slice everything into ribbons.

"No, I don't need it washed, just pressed!" Sylvia shouted, grabbing her underwear from my hands.

"No, Ashley, it says *hand wash separately*! SEPARATELY! You know, each *piece*!" Donna's baffling logic still stuns me.

"It's cashmere, Ashley! That's not cheap," Debra shouted, hysterically. Like she cared about price shopping. Well, actually, she did care. If something was on sale, it typically wasn't good enough for her.

I put all their pet clothes down carefully, took a step back from the crazy and said, dryly, "I'll be here all night." But they didn't hear either of my meanings.

"Well, do mine first," said Debra. "I'm older."

"Mo-om," whined Donna.

Sylvia thrust her garment back at me. "Ashley, I'm warning you. Don't incite my daughters." I nodded, just barely enough for her to think I was obeying. But Sylvia was oblivious. She was focused on her daughters, her eyes unusually lively, even moist with excitement.

"Now girls," she said to The Girls. "Time to get some beauty sleep. One of you is going to win the pro-omm! I just know it!" She was practically singing. The Girls caught her energy and began to bounce. "Enough with this... *sibling rivalry*," Sylvia said, shooting her eyes at me but speaking with an off-hand tone as she herded them out of the room, "we just never used to have so much of it before, did we? Did we?" The Girls were giggling now, but I'd caught the verbal dagger. With my stomach. And, *win the prom*? Seriously? I wondered: *do people even* care *about being prom queen and king anymore?* If so, I was totally out of that loop. But then again, I was out of most loops.

The laundry room door swung shut behind the three of them. I went back to folding towels (in thirds, of course), tuning back in to the comforting rhythm of a zipper hitting the insides of the dryer. I was glad to have them out of my space again. I soothed myself with rationalizations that I really didn't mind doing all this laundry, or all the other chores that kept me so busy; I like having a purpose, and I like to see results. I still do. (Linda says I might be a little OCD, and maybe I am, but at least it's my *own* standard of perfection. She and Professor März helped me understand the whole sibling rivalry thing better, too.[ii])

But just as I was starting to relax, Sylvia stuck her head back in, her voice weirdly sweet and flowery and fluttery, which should have made me suspicious right off the bat. "Oh, and make sure my silk blouse is neat, too," she said. "I want to make a good impression on Coach Pupkin. We have a very important meeting tomorrow. He's head of the *prom committee*, you know." Like I was supposed to be impressed. Like I cared that the next night was prom night.

As the door swung behind her again, I noticed something. When I moved Debra's cotton-candy Betsy Johnson cashmere shrug, the phone was under it, sinking into Donna's pile of fragrant undies. I picked it up and it rang in my hand. Right there in my hand. Sylvia's footfalls on the stairs paused for a moment, and I answered it quickly so she wouldn't come back into the room. I wanted her to think that one of the Girls had picked it up.

To my astonishment, the phone was for me.

3

MISS ST. HELENS ERUPTS

I picked up the phone and said *hello* really quietly, assuming it would be some giggly friend of The Girls, but was surprised to hear a somewhat familiar-sounding voice on the other end: deep, rich, and male.

"Oh. My. God," the voice said. "Is this my Ashley Ellen?"

"This is Ashley," I said cautiously. No one had called me by my full name since—well, since Dad died. "Who's calling?"

"It's me, Harry."

"Harry."

"Your Uncle Harry. You know, Harry, your Godfather."

Now, a bell was ringing. One of those gigantic church bells, like the Liberty Bell, like a gong going off in my head. I called him uncle, but he wasn't really my uncle. He had been my mom and dad's best friend when I was a kid. I hadn't realized, at the time, that he was also my godfather. I just remembered him as part of the scenery. So I started sputtering like an idiot.

"Harry...um...oh my God. Father...I—I remember you...I wondered what happened to you...I haven't seen you since my mom...." memories flooded my mind...playing "Alley-Oop," being tossed through the air upside down...walking holding hands between him and my dad, shouting

"ONETWOFREESWING!" ...dancing on his toes at a Christmas party...sitting with him at my mother's funeral...being mad at my dad when he didn't invite Harry to his and Sylvia's wedding...missing him, barely glimpsing him at my dad's funeral. I said, "What happened to you?"

"You poor doll," Harry said, his voice sounding like he was remembering, too. "Well, a couple of things happened to me. One: your stepmom kind of took a dislike to me. I think because of two: well, let's just say you could call me Harry God*mother* as well."

"Ummm," I said as he laughed heartily. "Okay," I mean, how are you supposed to respond to something like that, when you're seventeen and talking to a grownup (who's practically a stranger now) and you were raised to be polite? I was not sure what he meant. Fortunately, Harry did all the talking. He started telling me about my mom, and how great she was, and how my voice sounded just like hers. It felt so good to be able to talk with someone about something that felt normal! I had never really even been allowed to mention my mom in this house. *It will just upset your father*, Sylvia had insisted at first; then it became simply another rule to follow. "Harry...," I just had to ask, "Why haven't you called me before?"

"Honey, I call maybe once a month," he answered, "and I have been for years. They keep saying they'll give you the message. I thought it was *you* not wanting to talk to *me*." This news stunned me. I had no idea. How many other family friends were out there, trying to connect with me? I pulled a pair of skinny jeans out of the dryer. Their name: *Guess?*

Just then, the line clicked and I heard an extra-breathy version of Debra's voice. "Is it for me?"

I lifted my voice to sound like Donna's, hoping like heck she'd buy it, so I could continue my conversation. "Nope."

"Well, I'm *expecting* a call," Debra said, dropping her sexy voice and changing to her big-sister show-off voice. "From my *prom* date." She clicked off.

"Prom date?" Harry said. "Oh, my. Are you going?"

I couldn't help but snort. Not that I hadn't thought about going, but for God's sake, what would I wear? It's not like Sylvia would ever take me shopping. I was thinking about sewing two or three of Debra and Donna's old gowns from the Goodwill box together, but when would I find the time for that? Harry listened while I said all this stuff. Of course, I said it like I don't care. Totally a defense mechanism. Then he asked me how I got on with The Girls. I held back a snort, this time, and then took a breath, and rather than going into the scene with the underwear, just told him there was a little sibling rivalry. But now it was his turn to snort.

"OH, you are TOO KIND!"

"Well, I try to be understanding," I said, a little defensively; I really wanted to make a good impression on him. The truth is, I always try to make a good impression on everyone. I had never, ever, told anyone, at that time, what really went on at home or how I felt about my stepfamily. On the outside, it looked like we all got along just fine. So I said, very thoughtfully, "They're all right. They just act a little insecure sometimes." But Harry would have none of it.

"You can't be serious. Are you defending them?"

"What do you mean?" I asked. I knew what he meant.

"I mean, they are *awful* to you. I know that. I hear what goes on when I call. Sometimes they put the phone down and walk away, and I'm hanging there, helpless to do anything while they pick at you in the background. That's GOT to get to you darling."

I didn't feel comfortable with the way this conversation was going. I would have much preferred to keep talking about my mom. "Well, I try and stay above it," I explained. I had forgotten: that's not the kind of person Harry is.

"Girlfriend, NO. Get INTO it! You've got a right to your feelings." I leaned my head against the fogged-up window, focusing on the cold spot on my forehead, and struggled with this idea. No one had ever really said that to me before. Inside, my well-folded stacks of emotions were suddenly feeling like piles of dirty laundry.

"Ashley, give it a try. It doesn't have to be a big deal. Take two minutes, by the clock. Just get it out, don't keep it inside! Go ahead and BITCH your heart out."

I laughed out loud. “Harry! I’m not that kind of girl!” Harry laughed, too.

“You know what I mean.”

“I just hate that word. It’s demeaning towards women. But everyone uses it these days. Girls use it to be funny. Even guys use it with each other. Even little kids. Even on TV. And no one seems to mind.” There was a pause on the other end of the line.

“Ashley, darling, you’re thinking of it as a noun, see? I’m thinking of it as a verb. Bitch is a verb. To bitch is to complain. That’s all.”

“No one likes a complainer. I should know. I live with three of them.” I chuckled...then realized I’d let my first little bit of bitching out!

Harry, of course, was delighted. “There you go!” I laughed at myself.

“I know it’s hard for you,” he said.

“It is.”

“Your mother taught you not to speak ill of anyone.”

“She did.”

“Your mother, god rest her soul, was a bit of a doormat.”

I gasped. *How could he say that?*

“She *was*! She was the sweetest thing in the world, but your dad was the boss of her!” I had to stop and think about this. There was a rushing sound in my ears.

“Harry, I thought you were her friend.”

"I was the only one she could vent to, I knew her pain!" Now I understood. I wanted to ask him a thousand questions. But he said, "so try it, darling. Nothing bad will happen."

Still thinking about mom, I doubted Harry on this one. I could imagine a lot of bad things happening. Should someone pick up the phone, I would never hear the end of it. Still, I knew I had a lot in common with mom. And if my mother trusted Harry...

"Two minutes," he promised. "That's all it takes."

I took a deep breath and did my best. (I always try to do my best.)

"I always try to do my best," I said. "It's not like I don't want to help. I do, I really do. But sometimes it seems like nothing's good enough for them." Instead of more words, a sob came out next. The "sibling rivalry" comment from Sylvia had really gotten to me.

"Okay, honey," said Harry. "Deep breath. Let it all out." I focused on his voice and followed his directions. I started with the Spanx incident. Immediately I felt a little better, then started speaking randomly, intellectually, articulately, feeling more like myself.

"So, I guess it's like this: Sylvia's expectations are pretty low—she doesn't think I can do anything, even though I do a lot—but her standards are ridiculously high. Nothing less than perfect even comes close to being okay. She can always find some picayune detail that minimizes the hard work I've done. And The Girls either argue with her, blow her off, or take up her issues. Once Donna even told on me when I was using the wrong mop on the kitchen floor—like she'd ever picked one up, herself."

"Huh!" Harry was indignant.

"And once—you won't believe this—Debra even made me take care of her Nintendog, this adorable computer program that's supposed to teach you responsibility. Of course, having real responsibilities, I couldn't bother to pick up the stupid toy every half hour, and the puppy with the big eyes destroyed some furniture, or left a pool of virtual pee, or starved to death, whatever, who cares, it's not real. But Debra told Sylvia on me and of course Sylvia came down on me for having broken my commitment. What a hypocrite. She never does what she says she's going to do, at least not if it's something for me."

Harry was a great listener. He just kept asking for more. I let it all out! I told him what slobs they were, how I was constantly picking up after them, how they were always losing things and asking me where they were. As I talked, the cold fear in my stomach turned to warmth, and the easier it was to say more. The words tumbled out with enthusiasm, surprising me with their ease. I enumerated my chores in great detail and with time frames: laundry, cleaning, cooking. I gave half a dozen more examples of how incapable the three of them were of change, even with simple things like toilet-paper, lightbulbs, and kitty litter, and how cooperation was not in their vocabulary. I felt absolutely purified by the words rushing out of my mouth, and scrubbed my memories harder, emptying out every corner of frustration I could find. The half-eaten candy bars. The sticky floors. The gum wrappers "hidden" in couch cushions. The hair in every drain. The effing (effing, I have come to like that word; I think of it as a short version of "*eff*ectively emphasiz*ing*"...) lost keys, lipstick lids, stockings, earring backs, and sometimes homework. Styrofoam cups with teeth marks. Effing everywhere. And on top of the work they made for me: the snide comments.

"Lord," Harry said, truly sympathetic, when he could finally find a break in my stream of words. "How do you keep going, Ashley?"

I took a deep breath and thought about that question; the answer came to me readily, since I always worked to cultivate a very careful focus on the future, my present being what it was. I was just a year away from turning eighteen, and had sent in college and university applications to no avail, though I kind of had my heart set on Castleton, where my parents had met. "I have dreams," I said, somewhat dramatically, "but I'm not just a dreamer; I'm determined." And so I was. I stayed up late to finish every assignment and get extra credit, and if I'd been able to spend a little more time at school, I could probably have been Valedictorian. Harry asked if Sylvia noticed or cared, and I got a chance to snort again. "She bought a cake once when Debra managed to get an 'A '" I said. "Donna was so jealous. And oh by the way, it was an 'A-minus.'"

I finally confessed to Harry my darkest thoughts from my darkest hours, when I'd go to bed exhausted, fingering the frayed satin hem of the grass-green wool blanket that had gone with my family on every camping trip I could remember; it still had that old-tent smell, which made me think of dirt and gas stoves and the back of a car—and I'd escape to those places in my mind. I'd imagine the Hills when I was gone, eating cold, dry cereal out of dirty dishes for breakfast in their wrinkled, stained, cashmere track suits. I'd imagine Donna saying she missed me, then Sylvia would start blaming me for how dirty things had gotten.

"What! A! Bitch!" Harry said. I didn't know if he was talking about Sylvia, or me for thinking that, or impressed with my incredibly cathartic rant. Either way, we both started laughing hysterically. I had to wipe my face. My eyes were leaking all over the laundry.

(But for the record, I am still a nice lady who doesn't like to hear that word used about women who don't deserve it.)

Sylvia must have figured out I was talking on the phone. I could hear alarm in her voice when she called down the stairway, "What are you doing down there? I need my girdle by five!"

"Speaking of bitches...." Harry kept laughing.

"Yes, Sylvia," I called politely, resting my hand lightly over the receiver. Then I whispered to Harry. "Ironing a girdle! How pathetic is that?"

"Oh, right! You're in the laundry room!"

"Yes, did I mention that?"

"Absolute perfection." And then a long silence.

In the silence, I remember a fleeting sensation of gripping desperation. Was Sylvia coming? If I had to hang up the phone right now, I could lose this connection, which I now knew I *had* to keep. It was like having my mom or dad, silently, on the line. "Harry," the scared child part of myself cried out, my voice louder than I intended.

"I'm still here, honey. Not going anywhere, no way. Just thinking. And I know you don't have much time. So go slide open that closet where the water heater lives, and look way up on that shelf above it, and tell me what you see."

I had worked in that room every afternoon for four years, now. I must have cleaned it, reorganized it, five or ten times. But I had never looked inside that big box on the top shelf. It was old, from the fancy, old-fashioned department store downtown, with big loopy letters on it, "Grimm's;" tied with a faded red ribbon. I blew a little dust off the top. "An old Grimm's box," I said.

"Oh! Thank heavens it's still there!"

"What is this?" I had to hunch up my shoulder to hold the phone on my ear while I eagerly untied the old bow. Inside, under some tissue paper, was vintage silk taffeta with a beautiful pattern: dark purple and blue flowers outlined in black against a background of glossy green leaves. The inside of each flower was bedazzled by a few tiny glass rhinestones in three colors: green, yellow, and black. I lifted the gown by the wide, angled, velvet straps, and a voluminous skirt blossomed into life as it came free of the box. "Oh, my God," I breathed. I suddenly realized what I was holding: my mother's prom dress! "I've seen this in a photo, Harry!" I couldn't believe Sylvia had somehow missed it.

"And now you've got a gown," he said. I opened my mouth to say thank you and no, I don't think so, but instead sputtered and stuttered instead like one of those antique cars starting up. He didn't notice. I could hear him, on the other end, getting all gushy on me. "Prom night... here you come!"

"But Harry," I protested, "I can't go, honest." He couldn't possibly understand.

"Please don't tell me you have too much work to do."

"Well, obviously I do, but..."

"After that epic bitch session?"

"Doesn't change the fact of finals," I said, "and it doesn't change the fact that...." How could I say this? I struggled for a moment, then finally got my real reason from my brain to my mouth. I said, flatly, "I can't go. I don't have shoes."

"Oh, that can't be too hard," he said. But Harry had never seen my feet. How could I explain? I had to try.

"Yes, it could be that hard," I insisted. "You missed my big growth spurt between fifteen and sixteen."

"Oh?"

"It took place entirely below the ankles."

Now, I know what you're thinking: *No foot in the kingdom could fit in Cinderella's tiny glass slipper.* I know in the legend the thing that truly sets Cinderella apart, in the end, from all the other women, was the fact that her feet were so dainty and unique. Like her, I am different because of my feet, but in the opposite way. The only thing dainty about my feet is the nail on my baby toe.

My feet started growing a few months before Dad and Sylvia got married. Sylvia had ordered satin shoes for Debra, Donna and I, dyed to match our bridesmaids dresses, but the morning of the wedding, they no longer fit. The Girls convinced me to wear them anyway. I toughed it out on the ride to the church and the walk up the aisle, but the pain of standing through the ceremony was so blinding I passed out. Which caused waaay too much attention to be focused on me, and embarrassed all of us but my dad, who was cool about it. I completed the ceremony barefoot, but couldn't go into the restaurant for the reception. No shirt, no shoes, no service. Dad gave me some money to go to the drug store and buy some flip flops. Sylvia has never forgiven me.

Over the next few months, those really busy months of The Girls moving in and Sylvia redecorating, my feet kept growing. I burned out on shoe shopping because it filled me with self-loathing. Years later, I would adopt the habit of wearing my pants too long, with really high heels, so my footprint would appear smaller, but at that time I gave up wearing shoes, period, and started wearing flip-flops exclusively. My feet were flat, calloused, and always exposed. Debra took pity on me once and gave me some of her old nail polish, so that helped a little. But by sixteen I was a size thirteen. Standing sideways, I looked like a capital 'L.' Kids at school called me Bigfoot, behind my back of course, but I heard them. Sylvia kindly called a plastic surgeon to see if I could have a foot reduction. (Not without having my toes removed.) Later on, in college, Nevada and Linda would lovingly say *no girl in town could fill my shoes*, but I would always tell them they were wrong; any girl in town could fill them. With hot water. And bathe in them.

A few months after my dad died, I noticed some of his clothes in the Goodwill box, which typically sat by the door until it overflowed or until I loaded it in Sylvia's SUV and borrowed the keys to make a run. Underneath the suits and pinstriped shirts, which still smelled like him and made me want to cry, and next to the plaid mohair sweater, which I kept of course, were two pairs of shoes: some scuffed black wingtips, and a pair of white tennis shoes, never worn. I was hauling the box out when I thought to check the size. Men's eleven. I tried the tennies on...and they fit.

So when I told Harry I had nothing but my dad's old sneakers to wear, he was speechless, for a minute. Partly, I'm sure, the way all people are when they see my face, and get to know me, and then one day happen to glance down at my structural support system. And partly, he told me later, because he was thinking about when he and my dad went out to get running shoes together, vowing to start being healthier. But then they never ran in them. "Those *Just Do It* ads," he explained, "always made me feel guilty I couldn't just do it."

Just at that moment, Sylvia started calling down the hallway again. I was sure she knew I was on the phone. I heard the creak of the stairs; she was coming. Just at that moment, I smelled scorched polyester; I turned my head to see the iron sitting where I'd left it when I had turned to the closet to find the dress. I righted the iron and shoved the dress in the closet and closed the door while whispering a quick good-bye to Harry. Before he hung up, Harry said three magic words that changed something inside me. It had been years since I had heard them.

He said, "I love you."

A CAPITAL "L"

I quickly folded the smooth parts of the girdle over the scorched parts, and opened the laundry room door just as Sylvia reached the bottom of the stairs. "Oh," I said, feigning surprise. "I was just going to bring you this." Sylvia was dressed up to go out, wearing a very low-cut designer blouse, in a pattern that reminded me of the time I threw up French fries and a chocolate milkshake on my dad's plaid flannel shirt when I was six. But she was in a strange, elated, chatty mood.

"Thank you, dear," she purred, handing me her shiny Prada bag to hold, and then as she pulled the girdle on under her skirt, she started chatting about Debra and Donna's prom dresses and plans. "Clifton and Dudley are picking them up tomorrow for dinner, but I told them not to eat too much since they want to look their best and not have, you know, a pooch (here, she pushed her stomach in) when the Prom Queen announcement comes. One of them will win; I just *know it*! They come from a long line of prom queens, you know!" Here, she got wistful for a moment.

"We're going to be at the mall all day getting mani-pedis and waxing—Debra wants a Brazillian, but I don't know." My mom would have been horrified at the idea; she disapproved of grown women trying to look like little girls to be sexy. But that wasn't Sylvia's issue. "She's got her dad's skin and it might just make the hair grow in stronger and darker.... Anyway, I'll be gone, too, since I have to chaperone tomorrow night and you know, I just want to really enjoy this one day with them; it only comes once, and it really was the most wonderful day of *my* life." She straightened up, smoothed her skirt, and reached for the Prada bag. A manila envelope was sticking out if it; she pushed it down furtively with a weird glance at me as she turned her back and bustled up the stairs.

I had learned, a long time ago, how to not drive myself crazy by wanting things. The first Christmas after my dad had married Sylvia, we had met after school one day for our weekly date at the soda fountain, something we'd been doing since before I could remember. My dad had been distracted with work, and anxious about the family, and since the "steps" had moved in, this was practically the only time we ever had alone together.

"Are you doing okay, honey, in school, grades good and everything?" Now that I'm a parent, I knew what's behind a question like that. When grades aren't good—or worse, when they plunge, you know something else is on your kids' mind. But I knew my dad really, really didn't ever want to hear any bad news.... And that made it hard to talk, sometimes.

"Of course, daddy," I said. "I'm doing fine." My grades and chores were actually the only two things at that time I actually *could* seem to control. He didn't want to hear about my weight, my temperamental skin, my (non-existent) love life, my big feet, my story about how Sylvia told me to move my ass, or how much I was still missing mom. I sucked at my milkshake as I walked him back to his office, hoping he wouldn't comment on the fact I was wearing flip-flops with socks in the winter weather. "How are *you* doing, Daddy?"

"I don't know what to get the new girls for Christmas," he answered. "They're so different from you. Any ideas?"

"Let's look in here," I said, leaning my back against the door of Avalon Gifts and pushing it open. "I'm sure we'll find something." There were tons of things in there Debra and Donna would have loved. I pointed to a fancy princess telephone, a t-shirt that said "Lucky" on it with sparkles, and a calendar of puppies.

"For a teenager?" My dad was mystified.

"We're not all grown up yet," I smiled.

I found myself lingering over the collectibles cabinet. A six-inch glass Pegasus caught my eye. The horse had a strong, straight, noble nose with delicate nostrils, a thick, graceful, arched neck and luscious, curvy legs and belly. Her wings stretched forwards as if to gather speed, nearly touching at the tips. Her forelegs were bent as if she was jumping, and her muscled hindquarters were gathered as if she were about to explode free of the glass base.

"Like that?" I felt my father behind me. He kissed the back of my head.

"I love it," I said, smelling his Bay cologne, feeling his hand on my shoulder.

On Christmas day, there were three identical boxes with the Avalon logo on the wrapping paper. All three of us opened them together. To my alarm, Debra and Donna both got Pegasus figurines. That's so *not them*, I thought, poking the tissue paper in my own box, determined to be happy with my beautiful winged horse, even though I sort of had to share. But what poked out of the crinkly packaging was not a pair of wings, double drops of solid liquid, but a single twisted horn. It was a beautiful unicorn, with a prancing pose, but three out of four feet were on the ground. My prepared response did not come out right. I said thank you, but tears burned in my eyes and an ache burned in my stomach, a sudden, fierce feeling of missing my mom. I excused myself with a half a smile, feeling that rushing sound in my ears. Behind me I heard Sylvia say, under her breath, "Ungrateful."

Dad followed me, though, and explained through the bathroom door.

"We wanted to get you all matching gifts, but there were only two Pegasusses—Pegasi—left. To me, you're unique, like no other girl...so I chose the unicorn for you, instead."

"Thanks dad, I love it," I said, opening the door for the hug he offered. But what I really loved was him, and that he thought of me that way. And also maybe (he made a joke) as a pure virgin worthy of a unicorn's trust... (unlike the others, I guess?) Anyway, within two weeks there was only one Pegasus. Somehow or other, one of them got thrown and smashed during a sisterly argument.

The next year, the same thing happened at Christmas; three boxes from the same store—this time, Grimm's. Except this time, Debra and Donna got cute leather jackets; mine was vinyl. I didn't make a scene, I just smiled, listened to the rushing noise in my ears, and thanked Sylvia for thinking of me. Dad was no longer there to explain but I imagined what he might say. *To me, you're unique, not like a cow, but like a rare and special Nauga....*

I cried that night, realizing I would probably never get what I really wanted, ever again. I strengthened myself, thinking of all the people in the world who would never get what they wanted. I wondered how they coped—people who were poor, people who were at war, people who were in natural disasters or other sucky situations—and then I realized I actually *did* have some control. If I didn't *want* anything, then whatever I got would be a nice surprise.

This newfound Stoic philosophy got me through the next birthday and Christmas with grace and even happiness. As an added bonus, my unbridled enthusiasm kept the three of them slightly on edge. I was "in love with" Donna's old hoop earrings, "thrilled with" a book that Debra gave to me because she "didn't 'get' it" (and it turned out to be really good); I was "wild about" an acid-yellow sweater, hand-knit by Sylvia's sister, with one sleeve longer than the other. (The other two, by the way, got hot pink and apple green sweaters that both fitted and flattered.) I tried to focus on the giving, like my mom had taught me, not the getting. But it was getting harder and harder to do that.

So that evening, as Sylvia prattled on about prom night, I realized I was empathizing with her poignant feelings about prom, but in my own way.

Like Harry said: when would I ever get a chance to go to my senior prom again? Maybe I did want to go. Maybe I wanted, so incredibly desperately, for my life to be normal, just for one night. But maybe it would be better if I could be stoic and just *not want* to go, since if Sylvia got the slightest clue that I did, she'd probably find a way for me to be in Timbuktu, or at least in Castleton that night, twenty miles away. So I smiled widely, listened well, tried to ignore the rushing in my ears, and didn't say a thing.

4
MY FATHER'S SHOES

The next day, while Sylvia bustled The Girls around, I tried to keep a low profile. Every time I walked by one of them they'd ask me to do something. I was moody; I kept feeling flashes of anger, but I'm so good at not saying anything that, well, I didn't say anything. My head was full of questions. *Where had things gone so wrong? Why couldn't I just stand up for myself? Why did I care so much about those coffee cup rings on the furniture?* But mostly: *Do I or don't I want to go to the prom?* It didn't really feel like a possibility, so I kept trying to *not want,* but then again, I had that beautiful dress, and it was mine, mine, mine alone. It meant the world to me, and just thinking about it made my head sparkle with hope and excitement.

All day I kept trying to get back to my attic room, finding my balance between the slanted walls, breathing in the musty, cozy smell of the books stacked around the knee walls. Old books. Great Books. Piles of paperbacks. I had been planning on spending some time with Tolstoy as soon as I had the house to myself tonight, but now I wasn't sure.

I'd put Mom's prom dress on the antique mannequin last night, but early this morning thought it would be safer from prying eyes hanging on the inside door of the antique wardrobe. I hid it behind my Christmas gifts—the acid-yellow acrylic sweater and the spray-tan colored vinyl coat. I got to my room about four times on Saturday, between tasks and errands, and each time, I'd crack open the wardrobe to peek at the dress, smell it, explore the cheerful pattern with my eyes, feel the pretty rhinestones with my thumbs, and think about mom at my age.

I loved having a secret, too. When The Girls came in to lord it over me that they were going and I wasn't, I think I felt more smug than they did. To me, Debra and Donna looked ridiculous. Between them, there was enough makeup to paint all of my exposed walls. Their bangs were hairsprayed straight up, as if they were competing to appear taller than one another. Their gowns looked like they had come from the lingerie department.

"How do we look?" They jutted their hips out and flexed their legs, as if I were someone to impress.

I tried to give a compliment, really I did. "You look like wannabe prom queens," I said. Not that I would know. I'd never seen a prom queen before. But the fake boobs Debra had gotten for her eighteenth birthday did look spectacular in the silky dress she was almost wearing. My compliment did not come off well. Both of their eyes narrowed.

"Too bad you're not going," said Donna. She sort of sounded nice at first.

"Too bad no one asked you," said Debra.

"Too bad you have no friends," said Donna. The sarcasm was escalating.

"Too bad you have nothing to wear," said Debra, fingering my jeans, which I kept folded over a chair back for times when sweat pants were too casual. She spotted an old dress of hers underneath that I'd pulled out of the Goodwill box, and laughed. "Oh, are you going to fix that up?" Like I could fit into it. I had actually been waiting for one of them to throw away a second dress to sew onto it.

Donna grinned and said, "You'll need some birds and mice." Debra high-fived her, clumsily knocking over a stack of books. Donna sneezed her adorable squirrel sneeze, my favorite thing about her.

"What are you going to do with all your free time tonight?" Debra's wide-open eyes were made up to look as ginormous as the spots on a peacock feather.

"Maybe clean this dump up," Donna suggested.

I focused on my breathing, thought of my dress—being careful not to point to the wardrobe with my eyes—and started counting the seconds inside, until they left.

"Bye darling!" When Donna tossed her natural-looking curls, they moved in one piece.

"Have a nice time," said Debra, noticing that Donna was out-prom-queening her. She blew a beauty-queen kiss, so Donna had to, as well, as they stomped down the wooden stairs in their dangerously sleazy high heels.

I called after them. "Break a leg!" What I didn't say was, "Break your artificial noses."

Another beloved feature of my attic room was an antique sewing machine, which had been a present to my mom from my dad before I was born; she had used to to make a few baby blankets and some of those nice dresses I'd found in the box. It ran on foot-power with a treadle, which I pumped quickly now to finish stitching up a burst seam on Sylvia's chaperone dress. She showed up, next, in her girdle and pointy bra.

"Is my dress ready?"

"Yes, here it is."

"Help me on with it, will you darling?" It was no easy task. I had to stifle a laugh when I noticed the iron-shaped burn-mark on her bottom. Oops my bad.

"There." I said. "Looks nice. Have a nice time."

Sylvia's tone was unctuous, just dripping with charm. "You too, dear. Have a lovely evening. Try and get the kitchen finished, will you? It looks clean, but I found dust on the top of the refrigerator." Oh, for the love of pie. That really was a low blow. I'd worked hours on that kitchen this afternoon, even digging the grunge out of the joints on the faucets with a toothpick, even, making sure there was nothing, *nothing* at all that could be judged when we prepared tomorrow's victory brunch. But she won. She always won.

I sighed. "Yes, Sylvia."

"Be a good girl, now." She left, and a second later I heard the heavy front door slam. I settled in my book bed, and started to read *War and Peace*—it always makes me feel better. But I had only read a sentence or two when the words started to swim. Big drops of water plopped from my eyes onto the page.

I stormed down to the kitchen, my newfound anger returning. One night. Why couldn't they be nice to me for just one night? I wet a rag and swiped the cursed dust off the top of the fridge. Took thirty seconds. Big deal. On the way back up to my room, though, I wandered slowly through the empty house with the rag, swiping at this and that. I felt so alone. In my efforts to stem the comments and potential sabotage that would doubtless have come my way if I had showed any sign of initiative, my personal pendulum had swung from hope back to helplessness, and I had resigned myself to not going to prom.

I found myself in Sylvia's bathroom, staring at my limp hair, my baggy gray sweats in the toothpaste-spattered wall mirror. I smeared the spots around with my rag, thinking about getting the vinegar and water sprayer and some newspaper, and cleaning it properly, but... what was the use? Depression crept up from the soles of my feet, like evil magic vines twining up to pull me down. I struggled with, and succumbed, to the terrible self-talk, automatically bending down to wipe up the water on the floor from her shower, adding my tears to the puddle. I picked up the lavender bath towels. I folded them—in thirds—and hung them up again.

Creating order soothes me. And, as I mentioned before, there were sparkles inside my head that night. As I cleaned hair from the trap of the Jacuzzi Sylvia'd had installed, they gave me to a new idea.... Instead of just wiping fingerprints off the brass knobs, I could open the spigot, fill the bath with bubbles, and give myself a treat...like I used to in mom's clawfoot tub before the remodel.

Why not?

I pushed down the plug and opened the hot water tap, feeling possessed by the power of those two little words. *Why not?* I wiped around all of Sylvia's bottles and potions, opening up each one until I found a smell I liked. But why stop there? As the bath filled, I washed my face with some sweet smelling almond foam, pulled open her makeup drawer, opened a tube of creamy lipstick, and drew on a bright coral mouth.

Then I caught my image in the mirror.

Oh my God. What was I thinking? I looked garish and horrible. My pale face, tiny eyes, and stringy hair looked so much *worse* with that color. I wiped my lips, spat orange-red into the toilet two or three times, and flushed it. I stopped the running water, opened up the plug, and got the hell out of there.

As I lugged myself back up the stairs, the vines of doom came winding their way around my ankles again. I thought, maybe Debra was right. I don't have a date. There was only one boy I liked, anyway, and everyone liked Jeff Prince.

After fifth grade, we had gone to different schools, and by the time we got to high school, well, I guess we'd both changed. I'd voted for him for Homecoming King. Everyone I knew did, too.

It would still be fun to go, if only to see him in his moment of glory. I closed the door behind me, glad to be back in my cozy room. Outside the window, the sky was beginning to turn pink and yellow. I thought of Jeff and all my other classmates looking spectacular in the glowing light, as they piled into limos in their tuxedos, gowns, and corsages. I pulled out my journal and made some notes. My mom always encouraged me to write a little every day.

I wrote about Jeff. I was always proud of him, happy for him. He was a really good guy. In second grade, the music teacher had taught us to clap along, on the eighth notes and sixteenth notes—or tah-tahs and tee-tee-tahs—to this song: *Ice cream soda, lemonade punch. Tell me, who is your honeybunch?* Jeff had leaned over and whispered in my ear. *"I'll tell you who my honeybunch is: Ashley Stain Helens."* He had read my name on my folder...and almost got it right!

I wondered, with my pen, if he still remembered us. If he remembered that I was sweet, and kind, really, in my heart, without all this snarky drama that had taken hold of my life—sweet and kind and peaceful, and kind of fun, just like him. Wishing I could make the world a better place.

I shook my head and started slashing at the page with my words. *Who was I trying to kid?* If I went to prom, I'd probably just stand in the back and watch him dance with one of The Girls. Yes, they had somehow been nominated, and Sylvia was confident for some strange reason that one of them would win. I couldn't see that happening, but what did I know? They'd done their volunteer work, their leadership stuff, kept their grades up, whatever; they were good hoop-jumpers when they had to be. But still, I shuddered at the idea, feeling sorry for him.

And then I sighed. I didn't know what to do with this feeling, the feeling I wanted him. He was so adorable, but if I tried, maybe I could stop wanting him ... like I stopped wanting everything else. There was no arguing with the fact that we were separated by some pretty insurmountable obstacles. I closed my notebook, slipped it back between two stacks of books, and propped my giant feet on the windowsill against the golden sky. I tried to start reading again.

5
THE SOULS OF MY FEET

A loud HONK from outside nearly startled me out of my chair. I jumped up and looked out the window—I couldn't believe my eyes.

A shiny gold convertible Skylark with white-walled tires was pulling into the driveway. A statuesque woman with gigantic hair waved at me from the front seat, reminding me of these commercials for the Konvertible King that we all used to see as kids—although there was no wild animal in the car with her. The lady parked, checked her lipstick in the mirror, got out and adjusted her skirt, pulled a few giant vintage suitcases out of the back seat, and turned again to wave at me. Gleaming orange in the sunset, the lady was wearing a colorful dress with chunky gold jewelry, almost like something Sylvia would wear, but on her it was the opposite of frumpy, it was chic. She wore heels as high as Debra and Donna's, but on her they didn't look sleazy, they looked fun. I opened the window and called down.

"Hello," I called down. "Can I help you?"

"Ashleeeeeeeeeey! Look at youuuuuuu!" She threw her arms wide open. "Get down here and give me a hug!"

I recognized the voice: it was Harry.

The lady was Harry.

Harry was a lady guy.

As I tore down the stairs, I finally got his joke about how I could call him my God*mother* as well as my God*father*. Harry was not a small man to begin with. In high heels, and wearing a two-story wig, he filled up the foyer. His eyes darted around to take in every detail of Sylvia's out-of-the-box decorating style before they rested on me.

"Darling. How absolutely WONderful to see you again! My you've grown up *nice* — mmm, MMM, just the image of your dear mom. I think I may cry." He held an embroidered hanky up to the corner of his eye and sniffed. I had to laugh. "There. Now give your old lady Godpop a hand with these suitcases. Where's your room?" What, was he moving in? Harry talked and moaned the whole way up the stairs about how pretentious Sylvia's decor was. How *clueless* that she had gotten rid of the Art Deco light fixtures in the upstairs hallway and replaced them with those *tacky* faux candle-sconces with flickering bulbs. I opened the door to the attic stairs and he gave me a you've-got-to-be-kidding look. "This is where your room is?" He had to stoop to get through the doorway at the top. "Good Lord child, I was in the closet so long, I think you must be a woman after my own heart!"

Harry threw his suitcases on the bed and flopped himself down between them, poking the mattress, peering underneath. "I see you've adopted a literary solitude, how wonderful and romantic! But a gal as lovely as you *really* ought to have some semblance of a social life."

I could barely get a word in edgewise through Harry's banter. "So, what exactly are you doing here?" I knew the answer, in my heart, which was tap-dancing in my chest like Ginger Rodgers when Fred Astaire is nearby.

He ignored me, stomping over to the wardrobe in his clunky shoes. "I'm here to help you transform, of course," he said, spinning around and giving me the full sunshine of his beaming face. "You're growing up tonight, right? Well. I know the art of becoming a woman. I do that myself, at least once a week. And let's see what you've got in here...." He made a face at the sweater and the jacket, pulled the dress out, and practically danced across the floor with it. "Oh! It's like seeing an old friend! I wonder if it will fit?

"Did I tell you the story? Your mom wore it to her senior prom. We went together." He turned and winked at me as he lowered his voice and said, "I'll spare the gory details but let's just say *I* ended up wearing it home in the morning!" Harry hung the dress over the door and measured the waist with his large, manicured hands. "And I think it will fit you, just...so." He put his hands around my waist, squeezing through layers of sweatshirt. I couldn't help it. I threw my arms around him. I felt like myself, like I had when I was seven... although he felt very different, smelled different.... He picked me all the way up off the floor and crushed me in a familiar embrace (well, familiar except for the extra padding). It was like the other me with the terrible attitude of twenty minutes ago had been someone else.

"Oh my dear, I've *so* missed watching you grow up...." He put me down and brushed some hair from my forehead, wistful for a moment before laughing and starting to boss me around. "But here you've been locked up in a tower. Now I'm here to set you free. Are you going to put your gown on? Or just sit here all night like a bump on a log?"

I couldn't believe it was actually happening. I jumped up and down like a kid, then reached for the dress. Harry politely turned and admired the sunset from the window while I wriggled out of my sweats and pulled the rustling silk over my head. I shook out my hair, then stepped into my dad's clean white tennis shoes—(I'd thought about it all day; they'd be better for dancing than flip-flops and wearing sneakers with formal wear was all the rage now). I cleared my throat for Harry to turn around.

Harry stared through me for a moment, like I *was* a bump on a log. Then he shook his head and laughed a great big laugh. "Nikes with an evening gown? Girl, *just DON'T!"* I had to laugh, too. "Now take your daddy's shoes off, darling, and listen to what I have to tell you."

He turned toward the bed and started opening up his large suitcase. The latches snapped open, and Harry lit into a lecture I'll never forget.

"There is no such thing as a shoe," he began. "Don't believe me? Let me prove it to you. When I say 'shoes,' what do you think of? Maybe you think of your dad's tennies, or of high-heeled boots that could minimize your feet. Me, I think of my favorites, my 1940s Carmen Miranda wedges with the cork heels and the painted wooden cherries dangling from the ankle straps—*cha cha cha*—they're in here somewhere."

His suitcase was full of shoes! "So what is a shoe?" He continued. "Shoes are an idea. An ideal. An ethereal concept that we attach to any variety of...of *thing* we attach to our feet. Shoes don't have to cover your feet, or even protect your feet, necessarily, and believe it or not, you don't even have to be able to walk in them. The one thing shoes all have, though, in a special way that socks don't, is a *sole*."

"A soul?" I asked.

"I think you just said soul," he said.

"Soul."

NO SUCH THING AS A SHOE

"But I said sole."

"As in only—but shoes come in pairs."

"Don't confuse me, child! It's magical, isn't it?"

"What?"

"The *soul* or *sole* of a shoe. I don't think it's any coincidence they sound the same. We all walk our own paths in life, and our shoes give us direction! They give us definition! We wake up in the morning and say, Who am I? Who will I be today? A soldier? I'll wear army boots. A sailor? I'll wear deck shoes. A spy? James Bond dress shoes with daggers in the toe, as shiny as mirrors so you can see up the skirt of that beautiful woman you'll seduce in the midst of danger. Darling, there's a purpose to every variety of shoe, don't you see? Fuzzy slippers keep you warm. Movie star mules with a pouf of marabou. Your toes may sweat, your heels may take a chill, but—don't your ankles look lickable?"

I wrinkled my nose and smiled.

"Shoes tell stories of identity, Ashley. Think cowboys and indians. See, Native Americans wore soft-soled moccasins to sneak around in the woods, to be part of nature, to ride their horses bareback, in touch with the animal's breath and sweat and muscle. Cowboys, not so much in tune with nature as wanting to boss it around, put tough leather soles on their tall, protective boots so they could step on cactus and walk through cow pies. They'd strap metal spurs to their boots to creep their horses out and make 'em run. They put high heels on their boots to hold them in the stirrups while they threw ropes around things and tied 'em to the saddle. See what I mean? Indians do their mystical campfire animal dances, communing with their ancestors. Cowboys stand up tall and strut, all ego; even when they dance it's in a square!"

He did a little doe-si-do around me. Then he took my hands and pulled me down beside him on the bed.

"Ashley, do you know what it means *to walk a mile in someone else's shoes?* Empathy. How can you truly understand someone unless you start with their feet? *Wear their soles and you know their souls.* Is any of this sinking in?" It was sinking in. It was blowing my mind! And, no offence to Tolstoy, much more fun than *War & Peace*.

"So. Think of your own soul, think of how it makes you feel when you're really feeling like yourself, when you're really *knowing* who you are. What are you wearing? What's on your feet? Footwear is important—but you're never fully dressed without a smile, so if your shoes fit both your feet and your feelings, you're going to be a brighter light in this world." He finished, took a deep breath, and beamed at me. I sat there, soaking it all in. I could have applauded. I shook my head, instead.

"But Harry...." I had a serious problem. Two of them. "Look." I held my feet out in front of me. My pontoons. My giant sleds. My cricket bats with bangers on the ends. Harry looked at me blankly—at my feet, at my face, my feet, my face. Finally, he leaned down and unbuckled his own shoes—metallic blue, high-heeled pumps with tiny ankle straps. His feet were encased in panty hose, but I could clearly see the nails were neatly manicured and painted the same girly red as his fingernails—but with pink swirls on top. I had to smile.

"No, no, *you* look," he said gently. "Look closely." I peered again. There was something odd about his left foot. What was it? It wasn't ugly, it was...it was larger than life. It was...an extra toe, right in the middle! "Honey," Harry said, "sometimes what's weird about us makes us special." He crossed his 'special' left foot over his right knee, and then picked up my right foot and crossed it over my left knee, holding it to his, so our soles touched. A tingle ran through my leg, making me think of Kurt Vonnegut. Our toes and heels lined up. Our feet were the same size. “Don’t you get anything I’m saying? The Nikes?” I didn’t get it.

“Look.” He waved his hand at the bed behind him, where shoes of every shape and style and color spilled out of his largest suitcase. “My shoes are your shoes, and I’m going to help you find the perfect one.” All of a sudden, I got what he had been saying all along.

“Harry,” I said, “you're sharing your shoes with me?” I turned my head and looked into his eyes—*her* eyes, noticing how much *my fairy godmother* was blinking. False eyelashes fanning the air between us, eyelids shimmering in the late afternoon light. I shook my head and he was Harry in a wig again.

“I… I thought I should come in regalia,” he said, reaching a finger to the corner of his eye, “but maybe… maybe I didn't think through the makeup.” Tears were squeezing through the thatch of his lashes, and he sniffed. “No, I'm okay.” He took a deep breath and squeezed my hand. “Yes, I can't really believe it myself. But when you said you could wear your dad's shoes last night, I…well, I remembered we wore the same size.” He reached down and picked up the sparkling white trainer I'd taken off, and his makeup started to run freely. I reached for a box of tissues.

“I don't know, it's been so long, but it seems like it was…this sounds cliché…but like it was yesterday…mine are still white like this, too…we never did go running.” I put my hand on his back. Something like a laugh wrenched from his chest. “Instead he met Sylvia...oh, I miss him so much.” Now the tears demanded release, from his eyes and from mine. We wrapped our arms around each other and let the emotions come. It felt so good to share the pain with someone. His arms were so strong, and I felt safe for the first time since...well, since Dad.

He laughed into my shoulder, then pointed out the blur of colors on my skin. ”Oh, but this will never do,” he said, dabbing me with his hankie. He grinned foolishly, one of his eyelashes sticking out at an odd angle. “You have a ball to go to, Cinderella, let's get back to work.” We looked over our shoulders at the avalanche of shoes. “You'd better get busy,” he said. “Here, try these.” He chose a right gray satin pump and a left yellow lizard skin sandal. He laughed at my puzzlement. “I know they don’t match.”

I didn’t have a mirror in the room, so Harry was my mirror. I put the pump on my right and the sandal on my left. He cocked his head, squinted his eyes, and pursed his lips. Then he pointed at the sandal and took off the pump. He handed me a new contender, and so we proceeded. I switched out pin-up pumps, pumps with pointy toes, flats, slides, stilettos, and espadrilles, each shoe better than the last one. For the first time since I was a kid, I thought my feet looked pretty when I looked down, past the flicker and flair of my beautiful dress.

THE SWIRL OF COLORS

Harry talked a blue streak, all the way through, ticking off his talking points for each shoe on his fingers.

"Consider the virtues of the evening shoe. A stacked heel or stiletto elevates your view, so you're looking over the heads of normal, puny humans. Your legs grow longer, you look leaner, your curves are accentuated, and when you *walk*...oh, and when you walk, your hips swing a little, mmm-*mmm*! Makes men want to glorify your charms, darling! Oh, those *gladiators*! Strappy, sexy sandals! Men will want to lick your toes, darling. Lick! Your! Toes!"

"Harry, that's disgusting," I laughed, and he slowly raised an eyebrow, 'oh, really?' I shook my head and stared at my feet, but my mind turned to Jeff. I imagined *him* touching my toes, and I felt my cheeks flush.

"That's a nice color," Harry teased. "Oh, I know." He turned and scanned the pile of shoes, pulled out a pink patent leather mary-jane, and held it up to my cheek. I laughed and flushed more. "Wait, these might be better...." He held up a red vinyl ankle boot. "I'm sorry! I'm just kidding. But tell me...," he touched my shoulder, "Is there someone waiting for you tonight?" I shook my head no, but couldn't stop blushing. He slowly nodded and said, "Ah. Lucky guy." And then, nervous, "guy, right?"

Finally, it was down to two pairs. I liked the one on my left foot, a very elegant-looking spike-heeled sandal that had lasted several rounds, in the same green as the flowers in the taffeta—but Harry said it was too "CFMP," whatever that meant.... He liked the one on the right, a black velvet pump with a peek-a-boo hole in the toe and a bow that he thought made my large feet look 'cute.' I closed my eyes and walked around. The truth was, they both hurt. A lot. I sighed, and plunked down on the bed amidst the footwear. I was ready to give up and be thankful that we had gotten this far, when Harry opened his other bag. His face was silent, even reverent.

"I had a feeling it would come to this," he said. He pulled out a box, and unwrapped yards of white tissue from a shoe so shapely it seemed alive. I put my hand on his and peered into the paper at what I thought at first might be a sleeping animal from another dimension. The shoe was so divinely crafted it did not seem suited for the foot of a mortal, especially one as mere as me. But soon strips of soft green and violet suede cradled my foot like a slipper, curving upward in elegant spirals that twisted sensuously around my ankles. Glass beads were embroidered into the soft suede in a feather-like pattern that made me think of angel's wings. The sole of my foot was cradled on a thick pad of clear Lucite that swept in a wave up a few modest inches to an intricately carved scroll under the heel—like the translucent foot of an antique chair. My toes peeped out modestly between two overlapping bands of beaded suede, finished off with two pinched glass buttons that looked like tiny crystal candy kisses.

“It's a genuine Arpad concept shoe,”—I looked a question at him—“recreated illegally by a Balenciaga craftsman for himself...in his own size,” Harry whispered. “Nineteen thirty nine. The guy was a wizard with early plastics and all sorts of materials, sought after by all the great designers of the time. A real eccentric, who cherished the independent life. You should have seen his collection. He gave me these on my twenty-first birthday. I lived with him for a year in Barcelona after....” Harry's voice trailed off. After what, I wondered. Later, I did the math and figured out the moment the happy threesome of friendship he’d shared with my parents had become a twosome plus one around that time. One lonesome one who went off to Europe to figure out who he really was.

Memories played over Harry’s face as he ran his thumbs absent-mindedly over the exquisite beadwork. “Know what he said to me?” He didn’t wait for a response. “Keep your feet on the ground, and your head in the stars.” He held the shoe up to the light. It sparkled.

“Here. Try them both on at once.” He slipped it onto my foot. “It’s meant to be, darling,” Harry said, choking up. ”You can't fight magic!” I stood up and looked at him with surprise.

“They’re comfortable,” I cried. *How can that be?* My feet look so... so *curvy* in them.”

"They're not shoes, they're *art*," he cried. Then we both gazed at my amazing, sexy feet, wings on my ankles, ready to fly.

"Now STAND UP, girl, confident." Harry's voice rose again, full of passion. "You're radiant. You're the woman of the hour." He clutched his chest and swooned. "They're so dramatic! Ah, glorious! Magnificent!" I spun. I felt gorgeous. "Don't forget the source of all your power now—it's not the shoes, it's Mother Earth. Nature's gift to *you*. And all who know you! Draw it in, girl, from the *souls* of your feet!"

I took off the dress and shoes, and put on my robe. We snuck down to the Girls' bathroom—which was much more fun with him than it had been alone—and this time I did *take* that bath! "Soak until just before your fingers get pruny," he ordered, "and then scrub your feet while the water goes out." When I came out, he gave me the royal treatment: a blow-dry and set, a pedicure, a manicure, and makeup. I had been a little nervous about the makeover—I mean, I never wore makeup, and didn't want to show up looking like a clown in face paint. But Harry (who had fixed his own face while I bathed) insisted the transformation would have to be dramatic.

"Ashley St. Helens, I am going to make you look like the princess you really are!"

We joked about being a warrior princess, as was becoming the fashion in all the movies, but as the hot air from the blow dryer stormed my head and face, I felt more like a worrier princess. I was trying to get my mind around things. When he was done putting the hot rollers in, Harry saw the look on my face and shut the power off.

"What?"

"Nothing."

"What?"

"You're being so nice to me."

"And?"

"What if I ruin the shoes? Or the dress?" I sighed then, and Harry read my sigh correctly to mean, "What if I don't know how to stand, how to act, what to say? Would I fit in, wearing this old dress? Would anyone talk to me?" The hot rollers came out and he deftly fluffed and pinned my hair.

"Look, Ashley, I happen to know that you've found yourself in a position that abuses your sweet nature. You just give and give. What would you think of doing some *take*?"

"Take? Like what?"

"Take some initiative. Take a chance. Take a look around you at how you live! You can't let Sylvia and her snots run your life forever. They bring you down, they twist your energy. You won't ever have another senior prom. This is your one and only chance to have that experience, so *take* it... take it to the limit! So *what* if we get there late and you only have an hour? Make it the best hour of your young life!" I smiled. How could I say no? "That's my girl," he said, swirling a cloud of fragrant hair spray around my head. “Let’s make your mom and dad proud.”

“I also wish Sylvia could see you for who you are,” he murmured as he brushed powder on my eyes with a deliciously soft brush that gave me feelings. I didn’t want to say out loud what I was thinking—which was that I *didn’t* want to see Sylvia... and fortunately he seemed to be turning me into someone else. But when I finally looked in the mirror, I actually did look like me, just a more polished, grown-up version of me...with amazing hair and gigantic eyelashes like Harry’s. And some glitter. Lots of glitter!

As he worked, we talked and talked. He told me about his work. He’d had a brilliant legal career that went from being a habeas corpus petition specialist for a prestigious civil rights non-profit to directing a controversial innocence project for post-conviction relief, with all sorts of interesting human rights work in between. (Which, of course, made no sense to me in my heightened emotional state; all I understood that night was the “lawyer” part.) He talked about mom, and about dad. I told him all about school, and caught him up on some of our friends he used to know. It was SO great just to have someone to talk to like that... and to laugh! We joked about how he was my *Harry* godfather, my *fairy* godmother and—he pulled the collar of his dress aside a little to prove it—my *hairy* godmother, as well.

“I don’t care-y that you’re a fairy, you’re my hairy god-whatever,” I sung to him.

"Godwhat-e-e-ver," he sung with me. By the time I was ready to put on my dress again, I felt transformed on the inside as well as on the outside.

As we left the house, he said, "I have a present for you." I protested, but he assured me the dress was mine to begin with, and the shoes were most decidedly a loan. He reached into the dashboard and handed me a box. Inside was a simple gardenia blossom with a pin through it. "You can wear it on your dress but the petals won't be crushed if you wear it in your hair." At a stoplight, we stared at each other, grinning like we were in love. "I'm so glad you're back in my life," he said.

I said, "Me, too."

"Ashley, I've been...." Harry opened his mouth, then closed his lips and pressed them together, just as the light turned green.

"What, Harry?"

"I'll save it for later. My dear...your destiny awaits." The familiar streets and neon signs flickered by, and I felt like my destiny had already arrived. With the dress smoothed over my knees, the magic shoes on my feet, the intoxicating fragrance surrounding us, and Harry taking care of me like, well, like a dad, or a mom, or both...I felt like I was in a world that was mine again. Harry had, in a few short hours, built a castle on the crumbling foundation my parents had laid. I knew in that moment that, whatever happened next, I'd have a well of love to draw from, for the rest of my life.

6

THE TOSS OF A COIN

We got to the high school at about ten thirty and cruised around the parking lot looking for a space. Harry pursed his lips as we passed by an occupied car with steamed-up windows. He peered through his eyelashes and stroked his chin, smiling and frowning in quick succession, then glanced over at me.

"What?" I asked.

"Nothing," he said, shaking his head. "You look marvelous." He licked his finger and patted down a lock of my hair.

He pulled up in front of a crowd of kids that were hanging out in front of the gymnasium doors to catch some air. He frowned again, muttering disapprovingly about their cigarettes, then smiled and said, "Madam, you've arrived." I opened the door and gathered the folds of my dress around my legs, being careful where I stepped with the magical shoes. I turned to Harry, unsure of myself for a moment, and he gave me a cool look, sucked in his cheeks and purred, "Knock 'em dead, kid."

I walked carefully, finding my stride, through the group of smokers, which had fallen silent, then through an archway made of pink and yellow and white balloons. The gymnasium had been transformed by the prom committee, and I turned all around to stare and appreciate their vision and hard work. Round tables draped with gold lamé were scattered with balloons, curling ribbons, and candy. Golden stars moved across the high ceiling, projected rays of light cut through wisps of fog. Giant painted windows hung from the ceiling, showing painted scenes of some faraway land in the sunset; gauzy curtains wafted around them, stirred by secret breezes from hidden fans. Clusters of students gathered around clusters of giant potted palms, talking and laughing, sipping peach-tinted soda from sparkling plastic cups, their faces sparkling pink and gold thrown from disco balls hung at various levels around the room. A huge banner, not the printed vinyl kind, but hand-sewn decades ago on yards and yards of draped satin, hung from wall to wall across the bandstand, proclaiming again its profound wish for each new generation in scrolling velvet letters: "Happily Ever After."

I wandered through the room with my mouth open, drinking in all the detail and trying to reconcile the well-groomed boys and stylized girls with the kids I saw every day at school in their jeans and t-shirts. Everyone looked radiant, happy, flushed from dancing or laughing, and a little dazed—just like me—as if no one knew what might happen in the next few minutes. Who would they see, transformed into someone else? Would they feel a touch on their shoulder? Would their favorite song come on, and would the one they wanted be by their side when it did? So this was prom; I'd made it.

I stood in the middle of the room under the star-sprinkled ceiling taking it all in, savoring the moment and feeling lit up by my success in getting there.

There was a subtle shift in the crowd around me as the lights changed and the music softened and stilled. Coach Pupkin was climbing the stairs onto the bandstand, followed by the court. The kids all loved "Coach P," who taught P.E. and led our squash team to the state championships year after year. He had wooed me to join the team in ninth grade. And tenth. And eleventh, even though he knew I could never say yes. He was not too tall, not too thin, and even now, in his black suit jacket, he was wearing his signature orange cap and a whistle around his neck. He played that whistle like an instrument, sometimes blowing a sharp blast, sometimes a low gurgle, always following up the alert with a word of guidance that everyone—not just the athletes—respected, as it was always given with keen observation and caring. He was a solid, predictable, and reliable pillar of our community. And yet, we would all find out soon, Coach Pupkin was not what he seemed.

Three guys held the elbows of two girls who teetered on the stairs—Debra and Donna in their nightgown dresses—

and suddenly I remembered who I was. I thought I had been kidding when I said they looked like prom queens—suddenly it sunk in that all of that wasn't just talk. Suddenly I could hear, again, everything Sylvia had been saying in the laundry room; I knew they'd been nominated but where were the other contestants? The two of them were wiggling like puppies, jumping up and down, holding each other's hands (to the dismay of their escorts), as if this really were a beauty pageant. If they had been anyone else, they would have been totally embarrassing themselves, but seeing them in this social sphere I realized, that's just who they were. I spotted Sylvia standing near the stage, making hand-motions for them to pat their hair, stick out their chests, suck in their stomachs, and smooth their dresses. Coach Pupkin glanced at her nervously as he moved to the center—something was going on here. He tapped the microphone, which howled back at him at first, then cleared his throat and started to speak.

"Ladies and gentlemen, boys and girls," he said—and everyone laughed at his trademark Disneyland opener—"it's the moment you've all been waiting for. It's time to announce those hallowed icons of adolescence, the King and Queen of the Prom." Suddenly I was aware of Harry in the doorway of the gym. I gave him a little wave with my gloved hand (his finishing touch—black satin); he must have found a parking place. He made a "chin-up-and-tuck-your-tummy" gesture and I smiled, jerking my head towards Sylvia. He followed my gaze, rolled his eyes, and slapped himself on the hand.

"As you know," spoke the coach, the microphone whining at him again, "it was very difficult to narrow the field of nominees to only three men and (ahem) three young ladies." He shot a nervous glance at Sylvia and mopped his brow with a small rally towel he fished out of the pocket of his black blazer (flashing a bright orange lining). "In the, um, *style* of—" he cleared his throat again— "democracy, you all voted for your favorites, and I must say, the tally was overwhelming. Three hundred and twenty-seven out of three-hundred and twenty-eight votes were for your new Prom King...." There was a drum roll. Two of the three guys shuffled their feet. The crowd was beginning to cheer. My heart was in my throat—I knew who *I* had voted for—

"Je-e-eff Prince!"

Jeff stepped forward, gracefully, and I hugged myself, laughing and kind of crying at the same time, genuinely happy for him and so happy to be there to see him win. If anyone deserved the honor, it was Jeff. He was really cute, of course, with soft hair and an eager dimple that appeared at just the hint of a smile, but he was also mature, unassuming, funny, cool, smart, really good at everything he did, and friendly to everyone. My stomach hurt a little with longing for him, missing our friendship, wishing I could stand closer to him. I imagined every girl around me felt the same way. He had ascended to rock star status when he'd gotten hit by a truck last year in Village City. He'd jumped in front of it after winning an afternoon football game, waving his crimson jersey; the driver swerved and narrowly missed the herd of runaway preschoolers chasing a black cat across the street. Jeff was on the Tri-State news, a hero. Signatures had filled his cast so completely that people had started putting stickers on it and they were layered an inch deep.

As the coach handed Jeff the shiny gold crown that had been displayed in the front hallway's trophy cases since 1929, I remembered the cardboard and glitter crowns we had made in kindergarten class. Someone in the crowd shouted out, "Speech! Speech!" Jeff ducked his head and his dimple deepened. When the applause died down, he spoke quietly into the microphone.

"Well gosh, I couldn't exactly vote for myself, could I?"

As the crowd cheered, the most incredible thing happened: Jeff looked *straight at me*. He was glancing all around the room, making eye contact with his adoring fans, and when his eyes lit on me, they came back. It was like "oh, it's you, hi," And then, "what? Woah!" And then he was just beaming at me, his teeth shining like shooting stars in the changing light, his eyes puzzled, his dimples dancing, and me just grinning like an Elmo doll. Then everyone on stage was staring at me. Then everyone in the crowd was staring at me. Then I felt my cheeks starting to get hot and my ankles starting to sweat under the suede and that rushing sound in my ears—but in a good way.

The coach, oblivious to my excitement, wiped his brow again and went on. "So, uh, moving along here...the choice of prom QUEEN seems to have been a more difficult one...Nevada LeBlanc, our front-runner, bowed out of the race at the last moment with a bad case of the stomach flu." He glanced again at Sylvia, nervously. "Aaaannnd...between the two remaining candidates, we have, um, a tie." Debra and Donna stopped hugging each other and started glaring at each other, not noticing the coughing and fidgeting of the crowd. "Three votes each." Their cluster of giggling girlfriends below squealed and clapped and whistled.

But Jeff ignored them. He leaned into the microphone in front of Coach to say something. A hush fell over the crowd. His dimple was gone; he was dead serious. And then the most miraculous thing happened. He spoke out loud. He waved a little wave at me, and said, "Hi."

The coach patted his pockets, reaching in here and there, pulling out bits of paper. Meanwhile, Jeff pointed at me and said, "How about *you*?" By all rights, I should have fainted right then and there. It was *so* romantic, *so* flattering, *so* scary, and my heart was pounding like it could burst. I felt like I was floating above myself, looking down on the scene.

"So. Um." The coach glanced nervously at Sylvia again, and kept speaking, shouting really, since Jeff was breathing heavily into the mike, waiting for some sort of answer, as if anyone could have answered that question. I stood there, rooted to my spot, unable to stop smiling. "The prom committee, or, ahem, the 'revered administration of the crown,' you could call it, decided to let blind justice choose our queen." The coach pulled out a shiny silver dollar and held it up. His hands were shaking.

"Yes, you," said Jeff, again, nodding, beckoning me now with his adorable finger, and there came the dimple again.

In the years since, I always deliver this line at this point in the story: "What's a girl to do?" And everyone laughs at my seemingly rhetorical question. But at that moment, I really had no idea. The coin went up, up, up, and I took a careful step forward in my awesome shoes that should have been in a museum. The coin came flying down but when the coach reached out he missed it; it hit the floor, ringing in the silence, bounced off the stage, and rolled into the oblivious crowd. Yes, oblivious; hardly anyone saw this but me, while I was seemingly floating above my body. Everyone was totally tuned in to Jeff, who stared at me with such intention I was mesmerized, and me, pink-faced, ear-rushing—but golly, I'd seen my self in the side-view mirror of Harry's car, and couldn't blame anyone for staring at me tonight!

My feet took another step or two for me. There was a smattering of applause. Debra's face fell. She jabbed Donna with her elbow. They both glared at me.

Someone to my left yelled, “I vote for her!”

Then everyone started shouting. “Me, too!” “She’s the one!” And just when my knees seemed to magically transform into stuffed animals, people reached for me, held me up. Hands touched my arms, pulling me, pushing my back, holding me up, gently guiding me to Jeff. Hands practically lifted me up the stairs to the stage. The coach shot one last glance at Sylvia, shrugged, and signaled to the band behind him to start playing again. Ana Sueño, last year’s prom queen, returning from college for this special moment, put something on my head as I walked past, but I barely noticed. Sparkling stars were shooting into the edges of my field of vision. All I could see was Jeff, reaching for my hands.

“Hello, gorgeous,” he said.

“Hello, yourself.” His hands were very warm and steady.

“You look fine,” he said, and I felt like I was in an old romantic comedy I’d watched many times with mom and dad.

“I *feel* fine,” I responded, as if reciting my line. But it was true. I did feel pretty fine, in a way I never had before. I felt pretty. And witty. And bright. The cheering crowd parted as we walked down off the stage to dance, and the band started playing the dreamlike *Fairytale Waltz* that had been played at our school's prom since the legendary class of 1929.

There are moments in everyone's lives when they might feel as if the current of a greater story has swept them up; when suddenly, without warning, their lives converge with destiny, and somehow the confusion of everyday life dissolves, and they know just what they must do. This is how Jeff describes the moment he saw me and crooked that adorable finger. I felt that way, too, but in a strangely passive way. Like, it wasn't my own action that mattered in that moment, but people around me suddenly knew what to do. And that, I believe, is what made my life a fairytale—not the coincidental details of shoes and godmothers and Pu(m)pkins... but the feeling I got to experience, of being chosen *just for being who I am*. And this was my wonderful fortune.

Wonderful not only because Jeff "discovered" me...but because also, at this point, it was time for Harry to stand up to Sylvia.

As Jeff and I melted into each others' arms, only half-aware that we were becoming legendary ourselves, Harry sauntered up to the shell-shocked Sylvia somewhere far away.

"My presence didn't cheer her up much," Harry told me later. "Of course, I came in all smooth, all *Sylvia darling, you're looking trim...ish. Swellegant party. Shall we dance? I can lead OR follow*. At first she didn't recognize me. Thought I was some weird PTA mom, maybe we had worked together on some committee. I said no, we had only met a few times; mostly we knew each other from the phone. Then—it was great to see her face, think Katherine Hepburn in *Guess Who's Coming to Dinner* but not so gorgeous—she figured it out."

"'Harry!' (Harry did a marvelous and over-dramatized Sylvia impression.) 'Why...who...*what* are you doing here?'"

"'I thought we might dance,'" Harry said. "'We can talk. I can lead *or* follow." He grabbed her around the waist and waltzed her around the floor...actually, it was more like they wrestled. Sylvia kept craning her neck over the crowd to try to see me, to find out who the heck stole her daughters' crown. But Harry held on tight, because he had a few things to say.

The two of them plowed through the crowd in time to the music, making a scene so memorable that people still talk about it to this day. I now think of that song as *The Fairytale Catfight Waltz.* Over the years, Jeff and I have heard our friends recount stories of being in the crowd at the prom and witnessing this epic lady fight/dance wrestling match/royal ass-kicking. Coach Pupkin, who watched it all from the stage, later said it was like watching Bette Davis and Joan Crawford fighting, and he wasn't even sure which one was which.

Harry shouted things like,

- "I couldn't believe my eyes when I saw her tonight—she was a shadow of what she once was, of what she could be." And:
- "When she was born, her mother entrusted her spirit to me—and that meant something...but it seems you made it your job to destroy it in every way." And:
- "She was such a carefree child, but now she carries the cares of the world. Of *your* world, to be specific, on her delicate shoulders." And:
- "You may have kicked me out of your life, you wicked witch, but you couldn't kick that sweet kid out of my heart."

Sylvia, by all accounts, mostly stuttered.

Although Sylvia had figured out that this tall, flamboyant lady was actually Harry in disguise, she somehow hadn't realized it was *me* in disguise who had ruined her plans for world domination. At first she didn't know what Harry was talking about, and couldn't quite grasp that he'd seen me that night. She threatened him, of course: "How *dare* you accuse me of all of this?" And he said, "How dare *you*?"

Meanwhile, across the dance floor, I was totally oblivious to all of this, aware only of Jeff's strong arm under mine, his hand firmly holding my back, and the way we seemed to fit so well together. With the tall shoes on, I could look him right in the eyes. Green eyes. Flecked with gold. He said he thought I looked familiar.

And then, just for a moment, the magic faded away, like when musicians stop playing in the middle of a song. I thought he *knew* who I was, but no. To him, I was just a mysterious stranger who arrived at a convenient time, to save him from the unpleasant fate! I struggled with my feelings, both upset with him and attracted to him, wondering what to do.

"You're blushing," Jeff said, noticing that I'd stiffened up. I looked down at the shoes and wondered what to do. Those tiny crystal kisses reminded me of Harry's words: *Don't forget the source of all your power now...nature's gifts...draw it in, girl....* Then, rather than blurt out my identity, rather than feel insulted, rather than pulling away and running home, hurt...I chose to smile brightly and look back in those delicious eyes. And make him work for it. A little.

"Of course I look familiar," I said mysteriously. "I've watched you grow up from a boy who likes to catch bugs and play baseball."

"You've watched *me*?" Excellent. Just the reaction I'd hoped for. Behind his flickering eyes, I could see his brain searching for files...."I still like bugs and baseball," he mumbled.

"Paper airplanes ring a bell?" He shrugged. "Spaghetti bracelets? Lego racers?" His eyes wandered up and to the right, as eyes do when the brain searches for a memory. "Finger paintings?"

"Of naked ladies?" He asked, eyes starting to come back into focus. I nodded.

"We got in trouble," we both said together. Suddenly he lit up like I was Santa Claus.

"Ashley Stain Helens!"

"Siegfried Jeffrey Prince!"

"Shhhh, no one knows my first name," he said, pulling me closer and looking around.

"I've kept your secret all these years."

"My honeybunch," he grinned, hugging me. "I still have the macaroni necklace you made me! But...." he held me at arm's length for a second. "But you smell so nice. And...you look so different than you do in AP Calculus."

I lifted an eyebrow. "Yeah, I don't usually dress up for math. Or wear flowers on my head." Then my worrier princess acted up: Maybe he likes the make-up, not me. Yeah, that made sense. Yeah, obviously; how could I have been so stupid to think otherwise? The vines of doom reached for me, even in my moment of destiny. This couldn't really actually be happening to me; I'm dreaming, I must have fallen asleep on my book back at home. I pulled away.

But he grabbed my hand. "Ashley, that's not it, I swear. There's something else about you tonight. You look radiant.

Amazing. Happy. You look like yourself. Even though you're wearing a dress. Even though you grew boobs—I mean grew *up*—without me realizing. And I can't tell you how happy I am that it's *you*. It means you're not just my ticket out of this mess. It means that I can dive in headfirst—well, if that's okay with you, I mean—I mean... I *know* you." The words rushed out of him as we stood together, the crowd dancing around us, like a dam bursting. "I had been wishing and praying that something wonderful would happen tonight. I like Nevada, I *love* Nevada, she's totally great, she's totally beautiful, and something might have happened, but seriously, everyone thinks we're the class couple because we liked each other in ninth grade... but she's like my sister, we're good friends, and we both want something real."

Something *real*. As much as this was all pretend—the glitter, the big hair, the fog machines, the fantasy of it all had actually coaxed something I'd always imagined into reality. I couldn't answer, I just put my cheek to his, and it was warm, and we danced. I closed my eyes and I could feel our two auras sort of settling in together. I could feel the winged ankle straps of the glass shoes clinging to my ankles with each step. I could feel the cool crinoline of my mother's dress slide around my legs. For the first time since I'd lost her, I felt ready to dream about being like her one day. I sent her and dad a silent prayer of thanks for sending Harry to me tonight, for sending me Jeff, for sending me love.

Jeff and I talked as we danced, catching up as quickly as if it had been weeks, not years, since we'd been as sweet on each other as peanut butter and chocolate. "I heard about your dad," he said with a sincerely sorrowful face. "Cancer sucks."

We flirted, suddenly feeling like grownups. We talked more about Nevada, who might have been Jeff's queen tonight. Jeff said they had both been wondering if they'd die virgins, and then I was really shocked. I thought everyone had sex but me, and then he said the same thing. Everyone's all talk, we realized. But then we thought about all the girls who'd gotten pregnant and we both felt lucky we had a little more time to grow up.

He reminded me of our vow, in second grade, to get married when we were twenty. I pretended to be shocked but of course I'd remembered it all these years. Twenty is still too young, we agreed, but it had seemed so grown-up when we were seven. I told him about Harry, but we couldn't spot him in the crowd. Jeff said he had to thank Harry for wrapping me up like a Christmas present. Even now, almost a dozen years later, I'm still totally giddy writing this. I have seen so many couples fall in love and then break up. I still think it was some sort of miracle of fate that our dreams of each other were reliable. Jeff grinned at me like an idiot for the rest of the song, and I grinned at him right back. His dimple deepened. He said, "I'm thinking about kissing that lipstick off your face." Even my feet were smiling.

I was halfway home before I remembered Harry. I should probably go back, I thought. He's my ride. I had rushed out of the gym in such a panic that I wasn't thinking clearly. I slipped off the shoes and ran like the wind.

My mind was such a jumble of thoughts and feelings that I didn't actually notice my feet slapping the pavement until I saw the creek path up ahead in the moonlight. I leaned into the right turn and felt bare earth under my heels. And then I started laughing. *I can't believe I'm wearing a dress...at full speed!* I glanced up the creek, where the full moon was reflected in the water, and my mind calmed. I slowed and looked back—there was no one chasing me. Catching my breath, I held my arms out to the side to cool my sweaty pits, which is when I realized I had been clutching only one shoe to my chest. How had that happened?

Jeff was leaning down to kiss me, Sylvia had screamed, scaring me half to death! "Who is that? Who is that?" Sylvia was literally clawing her way towards us through the crowd. Apparently she had figured out what was going on...but she still didn't know who I was.

From the stage, Debra and Donna were pointing down at us and screaming, "There she is! There she is!"

"I think I'd better go." I disentangled myself from Jeff and ran through the crowd to the gym's side door, where my Latin teacher, Mrs. Armor, was standing with a group of her devoted students. I paused among my classmates to carefully twist off the amazing shoes—I didn't want anything to happen to them, or to my ankles as I ran. *"Veni, Vidi, Redii Domum,"* I joked as I backed out the door. My appropriate use of the Latin Club motto, *I came, I saw, I went back home,* caused a few double-takes. I latched the door shut behind me.

The bolt of fear that had shot through me when I saw Sylvia was long gone; now my heart pounded from running. I trotted back up the creek path and peered up the street I'd just run down, but alas, the other shoe was nowhere to be seen. For a moment I fretted about what to tell Harry, but I knew that he loved me and things would turn out all right. But that thought led to the next, like electricity in a step-up transformer: I also knew, in my heart, that Jeff loved me!

This time I danced down the creek path, twirling so my dress flew out and the crystals caught the moonlight. I skipped; I started running again, loving the cool earth on the soles of my feet.

When I hit the bridge, my steps rang like thunder and I stopped to still the noise and catch my breath. The soles of my feet on the wood, on the path, on the earth, grounded me. I had taken this shortcut when I was a child, and after things changed, I always slipped off my flip-flops when I walked by the creek. I had brought all my sorrows to this bridge, and had cried so many tears over the edge. The trickling sound of the water and the cool shade of the leaves above had always made me feel better. I always found myself able, after a visit to the creek, to set my mind right about things.

I peered down at my toes, sticking through the railings of the bridge, and felt joy flow through my body, like the water through the reflection of the giant moon. I noticed all the ripples were moving in one direction.

ALL
THE
RIPPLES

7
THE STROKE OF MIDNIGHT

When I became conscious the next morning, the first thing I heard was birds singing somewhere. I lay with my face in the pillow for a moment, sorting out these images in my mind: a shoe that looked alive, an enormous door I wanted to open, my hand and Jeff's hand—which was memory, and which was a dream? When my eyes focused on the dress hanging on the wardrobe, I still wasn't sure; I remembered wanting to put it on...did I, really? Jeff opened my backpack and pulled out a key as big as a book. Then I spotted the single glass shoe on the windowsill and I knew... both dreams were true in their own way.

I pulled on my dad's old sweatpants and tiptoed down the stairs to the hall bathroom, where I laughed when I saw my morning-after face in the mirror—eyes rimmed with black smudges, pink crusted lips, and a false eyelash sprouting from my forehead—then remembered to go back upstairs and dig out my mom's punch bowl from under the bed. Sylvia had asked for it—okay, demanded it—for today's post-prom brunch. I didn't know what would happen now, but I was sure she could use my help.

By mid-morning, the table was ready and the buffet was set up, ready for me to put the food out, but I hadn't heard a peep from upstairs yet. Sunlight streamed in to the living room from the tall windows—I opened them to let air in, and then set about taking the slip-covers off the furniture. I frowned at my dad's old rolltop desk in the corner of the room, now piled high with papers. I thought about rolling it shut but when I started to push a stack of clutter, I heard Sylvia's voice screeching in my head not to touch her desk. Turning my back on the mess, though, everything looked calm and welcoming, like a home again. Like *my* home. I didn't really know what to expect next; I was just happy. I looked down at my toes, painted with pink swirls, and got an idea that I should maybe wear something pretty to the party.

I trotted up the stairs and changed into one of my mom's summer frocks. I was stabbing a pencil through my crispy, twisted-up hair, still poofy and shiny from last night—when I heard a car pull up in the driveway, then another car. Voices floated in through the small attic window.

"Good morning, Jeff!" It was Harry.

"Hello, um... I'm...." Jeff sounded baffled that the person who got out of the gold Skylark seemed to know him.

"It's me, Harry," said Harry's voice.

"Carrie?" Said Jeff. And then I heard him laugh. Then Harry's voice again.

"What did you say last night, all forlorn, when you were holding that shoe like a newborn baby? *No one could ever fill her shoes?* Well…try me!" I ran to the window and saw something almost as strange as the sight I'd seen the evening before. There was a middle-aged man in a sweater vest and an advancing forehead standing in front of Jeff, pulling one of his pant legs up to expose a length of flexed calf, a bare ankle, and a woven leather deck shoe on a pointed foot. To my great relief, Jeff held the other shoe in his hands. I sighed, delighted to see the shoe, delighted to see them both, delighted to see the two of them together.

"Okay, that's just creepy," Jeff laughed. "I'm sure it fits. Hi Harry."

"It was charming dancing with you last night," Harry said. I covered my mouth to stifle a giggle…What did I miss?

"I'm so glad you cut in when you did," Jeff said. "Dancing with you was much better than dancing with the stepmonster."

"Swear to God, that woman would have puppeteered you around the dance floor to get you to dance with one of her daughters," said Harry.

"Or both! Did you see how she shoved them at me?"

"Well, I'd just been puppeteered so I wanted to save you from that fate. That woman is stubborn," said Harry. "Have you ever tried calling this house to talk to Ashley?"

“Yeah, now that you mention it, but I stopped after a while because I got tired of talking to Debra and Donna.” Jeff’s voice trailed off at the end, regretful.

“I’ve got such news for her,” spouted Harry, “but I can never get through… and when I get Sylvia, it’s like she can’t hear me!”

Ah, suddenly something came clear.

About a week ago in the kitchen, Sylvia had stepped on some mashed potatoes with corn, and then was freaking out and blaming everyone who came near, spinning a line of logic that predictably made it everyone’s fault: mine for not cleaning it up, Donna’s for being the last one to eat, and Debra’s for having a craving for Kentucky Fried Chicken biscuits that night. (Oh, and by the way mine for not cooking something from scratch. Even though I’d offered.) It was also for some reason her “*effing* mechanic’s” fault (except she didn’t say *effing*…) for forgetting to put an “*effing* sticker” on the windshield six *effing* months ago to remind her the car needed an “*effing* oil change.” A few seconds into her rant, I knelt down with a paper towel to wipe up the mess (rescuing a Cheeto and a scrunchie from under the cabinet while down there), but then she lit into me about wasting paper towels when I could have been using a sponge. At which point I stared up at her blankly, since just last week she had gone off about me using a sponge on the floor when I should have used a paper towel. Then she shrieked, suddenly, that there was now some goo on her shoe, and shook her pointy white pump in my face. That was too much. I stood up and summoned the courage to say something, even considering working her version of the word *effing* in it.

Saved by the bell. Just then the phone rang, and Sylvia broke off her glare to look away and answer it. "Hello, St. Helens and Hill residence..." Her voice was suddenly singsong and professional, like maybe a teenage receptionist at a tanning spa. She chuckled gently and glanced at me and said, "No, I'm afraid you've missed her again; I'll give her the message you called." I gave her a curious look but she just listened, and her smile stretched tighter until she was talking through her teeth. "I'm sure I don't know what you're talking about."

And then she took the sharp tone of someone trying to rid themselves of a phone solicitor. "No, I really have no interest in that. Besides, I just don't have the time, trying to keep three teenaged girls clothed and fed, plus my extensive volunteer work with the King Phineas Food Bank, I'm sure you understand."

"No, I'm sorry, you're not hearing me, I really can't. No thank you. Bye-bye for now."

KING PHINEAS

"So I finally reached her last Friday," Harry told Jeff, leaning on the hood of his Buick. "But I got carried away when I heard it was prom, because, well fairytale weekends don't happen every day!" Harry was getting emotional, starting to laugh and cry all at once. “Oh! Did you hear what I just said! *Carried away!* Don’t you get it?” Jeff shook his head; he didn’t get it. “*Carrie D’Aweigh*! That’s my stage name! She’s a fallen Southern Belle!” Jeff still looked blank. My mouth was open. “I headline on Sundays down at the Teddy Wolf in the pink light district!” Now I got it. Carrie D’Aweigh is my fairy godmother. Carrie D’Aweigh is who danced with both Sylvia and Jeff at the prom.

“Harry Carrington,” I shouted, unable to hold back my excitement any longer. “Harry Carrie! Carrie D’Aweigh! My hairy, fairy god-whatever!” I sang our little song from last night. “Isn’t it a beautiful day?” Jeff and Harry looked up, big smiles on each of their faces. “Would you like to come inside?” I grabbed the shoe from the windowsill and tromped down the stairs again.

When I opened the front door, I had to sort out my second impression of Harry from my first. The outrageous woman who had walked in last night (Carrie) was nothing like this well-groomed, low-key forty-something fellow (Harry). He was a foot shorter than her, and shorter than my childhood memories of him, but was familiar to me now, an equally great surprise. “You look divine,” he said, in one graceful move bending down to grab the Sunday paper, handing it to me, kissing me on the cheek, and touching my head. “You have an eyelash in your hair, dear.” Oh, there was the other one.

Then Jeff stood square in front of me and stared, grinning from ear to ear. "Oh, it's you," he said, probably having the same disconnect with me that I'd had with Harry, since I'd un-transformed overnight as well. "Look, I have one, too," he said, nodding at the shoes we were both cradling, stroking them like puppies.

"They're so soft, aren't they?" I ran my fingers over the gentle suede and the cool glass beads. He stared and smiled and nodded some more. "Want some juice?" I finally offered. "Or coffee? Or tea?" They followed me into the kitchen and I reached in the cabinet for a mug, forgetting I'd laid out a beverage table with the punch bowl and the shining silver samovar.

"Champagne?" Harry pulled a chilled bottle out of the sparkling clean refrigerator, making himself at home as if no time had passed at all, as if it was still Mom and Dad's house. "I think there's an occasion. Oh wait, you guys are minors, I'm going to have to get used to being around the underaged. Good. There's some sparkling cider in here too."

I grabbed some glasses and pulled a pan out of the oven, the shoe still tucked under my arm. I looked in Jeff's eyes and offered him some food. "Muffin?"

"Yes, Honey Bunch?" Jeff teased, leaning against the counter top. Harry laughed. We trundled back to the living room and settled in to the clean, naked armchairs, sharing a celebratory mood. "Did you try that shoe on everyone in town before you got here?" I asked Jeff, who was now carrying his like a football. "Or just Harry?"

"Oh! Here! I should give it to you," Jeff said, handing it to me. "Or is it yours?" He shoved it at Harry.

Harry took both shoes and got up to place them on the windowsill nearest the door, where the sun was shining directly in, painting large squares of sunlight onto the old wooden floor. The transparent soles cast a curious rippling shadow in the square, and the carvings threw mystical swords of light onto the walls. Sparkles from the glass beads cast themselves about the room, and Jeff sang, "Aaaaaah," like a choir of angels.

"Darling, you wouldn't believe what a scene you missed last night," said Harry. "You left just before midnight. Sylvia never knew it was you. She was all, like, *who stole my daughter's crown?* and once you were gone, *Jeff, for God's sake, dance with my daughters!* And the band had stopped playing, and everyone was staring at her—"

"Aawwk-ward!" Jeff chimed in. "Especially since I was dancing with Harry."

"I even dipped him," said Harry.

"He dipped you?" Now I stared at Jeff. He blushed. Harry punched his shoulder and rushed on.

"In the silence," Jeff continued, "Coach's watch starts beeping midnight. Well, Sylvia forgets about us—"

"—and we stop dancing—" Harry pointed out.

"You dropped me," Jeff mentioned.

"—and she reaches into her purse."

"People freaked out—they thought she was reaching for a gun!" Jeff said, gesturing with his hands. "Some kids even hit the floor!"

"But no, it's a cell phone," says Harry, "and she dials a number and says, *Run it*, glaring daggers at the coach the whole time."

"Their eyes were locked," Jeff said, illustrating by pointing two fingers at my eyes, then his, then Harry's, then his. What on earth? Now I was remembering what she said when she came to put on the girdle...and the package in her purse....

"Then Coach starts peeling off his clothes!" Harry was nearly doubled over laughing at the memory. He stood up and started mimicking a strip-tease. "The orange cap. *Ba-dump.* The black jacket with the day-glo orange lining. *Ba-dump.* The whistle, even his Black Forest High wristbands—*Badump-bah!* He peels them off and throws them one by one at Sylvia's feet."

"The dude is buff," Jeff said. "And now he's standing there in jeans, a white t-shirt, his hi-tops, and his now-silent watch."

"Kind of hot, actually," Harry murmured to himself. "In a James-Dean-at-forty kind of way."

Jeff continued. "And he goes, glaring at Sylvia, '*I said what I had to, but it's over now.*' Then he looks up at the crowd and says, '*Party's over, kids, go home. And goodbye.*'"

Harry finished, "'*Effective immediately, I'm no longer the squash coach. I'm going back to being Jack Pupkin, regular guy.*'"

"No!" I couldn't believe it.

Jeff started laughing hysterically.

"What?" We both turned on him.

"I just got it!"

"What?" He had to catch his breath first.

"Come *on*, Cinderella," Jeff said, "Your *coach* turned back into a *Pupkin* at midnight!"

The stairs creaked. We looked up to see Donna coming down. She took one look at Jeff, made a little "eep!" sound and turned around to run back up the stairs, where she crashed right into Debra. They whispered excitedly and then came wiggling down together, pulling their scrunchies out and tossing their still-stiff hair around their shoulders. When they got near enough, their faces, too, became flecked with light from the shoes. One wore a pink sweatsuit that said "Pink" across the buttcheeks. The other wore a green sweatsuit that said "Juicy." Donna called out, "Hhhhiiii, Jeff!"

Jeff nodded and excused himself to find the bathroom.

The Girls were astonished and excited. "Go tell mom," Debra said, elbowing her sister.

"You go tell mom," said Donna.

"Tell me what," grumbled Sylvia, stumbling down the stairs behind them in her satin robe, hair frizzing uncharacteristically around her elegant shoulders. She stumbled past us, past the dining table set with the nice silver, into the kitchen—without noticing who was on the couch.

"There's coffee," I said to them all.

"Ooh, and punch," said Donna, discovering the beverage layout on the sideboard. "Ashley, this is so nice. Who else is coming to our brunch?"

"It's cancelled," said Sylvia, coming into the living room with the orange juice pitcher in one hand and a champagne bottle in the other, a glass tucked under her arm. She sat down hard at her desk, blinking away the dazzling pinpricks of light from the shoes. "Close that damn curtain." Then she looked up and noticed the company.

"Harry! What the hell?" She turned her head at the sound of a toilet flushing.

Jeff came out of the bathroom hallway and Sylvia jumped out of her chair, her tone turning solicitous. "Jeff! What are you doing here? Did you come to apologize? That's so wonderful!" She smoothed her hair. "Oh, now *nice* of you to come over! In spite of your rash actions last night, I knew you were a boy of character! Get him some food, girls." Jeff had no chance to reply because he was suddenly surrounded by The Girls, who were making conversation that required no effort on his part at all.

I served the spiced sausage strata, a favorite recipe of my mom's, which sent Harry down memory lane and (hallelujah) drew no complaints from The Girls, probably because Jeff raved about it. Sylvia hovered near her desk, thinking, drinking mimosas. When she lit a cigarette, though, the three of us girls exchanged worried glances—she never smoked in front of us—but Jeff was such a stabilizing presence that the mood stayed light. I introduced The Girls to Harry. Delighted to have a male guest in the house, they were surprisingly nice to him. We balanced plates on our knees rather than sitting around the dining table, and as we moved in and out of the sparkles of light from the shoes, it felt like a real celebration—even though no one knew exactly what was going on.

"Hey Jeff, remember that time you were here studying with Ashley in ninth grade?" Debra sat onto the couch next to Jeff. "You left these..." She reached her hand into the cushions and pulled out a box of Tic-Tacs. Jeff stared at her blankly. Donna lunged.

"Give me those! I found them first!"

"Sure, Donna. You can have them. Jeff's right here by me." She tossed the candy box across to Donna. She shook it. There was only one left.

"Oooh!" Donna glared and tossed the box aside. There was no room on the other side of Jeff; he was sitting at the end of the couch. She plumped down in an armchair with her food and picked up the morning paper from the coffee table. Then she gasped and coughed out some biscuit. "Oh! My! God!"

She turned the Town Herald Sunday Edition around so we could all see the front page. The headline read, "Black Forest Coach Stripped of Position." There were two photos above: one of Coach Pupkin with the basketball team, and one of Judy Garland singing. We all went, "huh?" Harry did a spit-take onto the chintz armrest.

"Black Forest High's senior P.E. teacher," read Donna, *"who led the Trolls to a state championship last year, was outed by an anonymous parent last week, who called for his resignation."* In unison with Debra she turned and said, "Mom!" Sylvia sucked her cigarette and shrugged.

I grabbed the paper and read on. *"Down at the Teddy Wolf nightclub, no one guessed the winner of last week's drag competition was Coach Jonathon 'Jack' Pupkin of the local high school—"*

Harry gasped. "S/he was *amazing*! The most sensitive Judy we'd ever seen!" He slapped his thigh. "I can't *believe* it! How could I *miss* that? I'm so good with faces! What an *artist*!" He grabbed the paper from me, now, squinted at the picture, then continued to read. "*'I can't believe he was juggling so many balls,' remarked one admiring judge when asked to comment on this story."* Jeff snorted. *"'It takes a lot to sing like that, to dress like that. And to teach six hundred students physical culture for a day job. It took guts, a lot of guts.'"*

"Who writes this stuff?" Jeff wondered aloud, frowning as he grabbed the paper to inspect the byline.

Harry glared at Sylvia. "Why would you DO such a thing, Sylvia? Of all the low tricks! He may or may not be gay but it's nobody's business to speculate!"

Sylvia slammed her champagne bottle down on the single square foot of exposed desk space and screamed, "We! Had! A! Deal!" To our blank stares, she spat out the words: "We had a deal one of my daughters would win!" Sylvia stood up so fast that papers flew off her desk.

"You... you *blackmailed* him?" Harry whispered.

"You *fixed* the prom?" Jeff looked like he wasn't sure whether to laugh or be furious.

Donna and Debra looked ashen, and stuttered through the logic together. "You mean—"

"—you *arranged* for us to be elected to the court?"

"You mean—"

"—we weren't nominated by *anyone*?"

"You mean—" They looked at one another, horrified, and screamed in unison,

"We're not popular?" They dissolved into tears and ran up the stairs, sobbing, a fork flying, grapes from the fruit salad rolling onto the carpet, under the chairs.

"Nice going, mom," sneered Harry, settling back in his chair and glaring at Sylvia. Jeff and I stared uncomfortably at anything but her. I thought about Nevada, and all the others who actually deserved the honor my stupid family had stolen.

Sylvia stared, stricken, out the window, her shaking hand pressed to her mouth.

Moments ago, the mood in this room had been delightful; now, waves of crazy were emanating from the corner desk and no one was speaking. I started cleaning up. Jeff studied the paper. "Photo source: Justin Case," he read, "wait – he's a private detective! My dad knows him! Now he's selling photos to the paper?"

"*I* sold the photo," said Sylvia, "to pay for his services."

"That's unethical," Jeff shouted.

"Well at least I gave him a photo credit," she retorted. "Besides, what would I know about ethics? I didn't go to college. *I'm* not the one with the law degree," she said, glaring at Harry, trying to make it his fault, perhaps, somehow? I could tell Harry was biting his tongue, not wanting to laugh out loud.

"Why would I need to? I was *prom queen*," Sylvia went on. "I had four marriage proposals by the end of the night! Everyone but *everyone* wanted me! But did I marry? NO! I leveraged my assets, managing my looks and social calendar and turning them *both* into a living over the years. I mean, when the twins came I figured out how to live on child support from *both* of their dads! It took me *years* of community service to build my reputation, and to find a man who could love and support me for who I really am, and give my girls the life they deserve... until YOU!" She glared at Harry, furious, then at Jeff, then at me.

With a shriek of frustration, Sylvia swept the contents of her desk to the floor. "Who the hell WAS that girl anyway?" She advanced on Jeff, holding the champagne bottle, having abandoned the orange juice several swigs ago. "You had no *right* to choose your own prom queen! All this *planning* and *hard work* by adults—and you kids go and do whatever you feel like."

"Sylvia..." Harry tried to calm her down.

"Children are so *ungrateful*! They need *so* much support, and it's hard for one person to do it all." She took another guzzle, and then went crazy about my dad, me, and her grief. Jeff just stared, his eyes wide. "It's just *impossible* when the person you *hoped* and *dreamed* and *vowed* would be there with you for the rest of your *life* not only comes with so much *baggage*," here she gestured at me, but was clearly appealing to Harry, "...and his constant memory of *her*, which is bad enough *already* but then he up and *dies* on you, leaving you in *charge* of said person, and so now rather than being taken *care* of for the rest of your life, you are forced to take care of her, and of that *memory* of his, and not *him*, but *her* face in your face, in your own house! But what's worse, it's not even your own house! In his will he leaves it in some *trust* for her and you have nothing, really, *nothing* of your own! You have no *idea*! It's too much! It's just too much! I work full *time* mothering these girls, there are *no* other options!" She threw herself back into the chair and sobbed on her arms.

Harry stepped between Jeff and Sylvia, cleared his throat, and took charge of the conversation.

"Sylvia," he said in a calm and businesslike voice, "there's something I've been trying to talk to you about. It might actually help solve your problems. I was trying to invite you out for coffee and do this the nice way, but you've blocked me at every turn." Sylvia kept her head down. Harry took a breath, looked right at me, and continued. "I found a letter from Ashley's mother from seventeen years ago, when she asked me, formally, to be Ashley's godfather. It said very unequivocally that if anything ever happened to both of them, she'd like Ashley to live with me."

"What!?" Sylvia's head shot up.

"What?" I stared, stunned.

"What does unequivable mean?" Sylvia slurred.

Harry turned to me. "Ashley, I have a proposal, I mean, a proposition for you. I was hoping to ask you this last night but events took on a life of their own. I know you're not a baby anymore but can I... I mean, will you... I mean...."

Jeff and I looked at one another, incredulous. He reached over and patted Harry on the shoulder. "On one knee, big guy, that's how it's done," and I laughed, falling in love with him just a little more. But Harry was now as worked up as Sylvia and couldn't even finish his sentence.

"It was a...a big decision for me, as you can imagine. I mean...becoming a mother? At my age?" Jeff and I cracked up. "Starting with a teenager?" Harry was now relishing his moment. He glared at Sylvia.

"Ashley, I was furious with Sylvia, who would never let me even finish my sentence," here he raised his voice, "which may have included the phrase, *'take her off your hands'* if I'd known how she really felt! I went on a research rampage for the next few weeks, trying to figure out how I could get you out of there without her consent. And I finally found out... I realized...."

"What, Harry?" I had never technically considered my legal status before.

"Ashley... you're an orphan. Sylvia never adopted you. You're over sixteen. You can be," he took a breath, "legally emancipated."

"Emancipated?" It sounded like the end of slavery.

"You don't have to live with her anymore."

I sat down, unable to stand for a moment, and stared at him.

"Ashley... if you want to... would you...would you like...like to live with me?" Harry stammered, blushed a little. "I could even adopt you, but the fact is in six months you'll be a legal adult. Free...free to be..."

Jeff said, "Free to be? You and me? Free to be?"

At first I hesitated, wondering what would become of the house if I left, but one look at Jeff's caring face reminded me of Harry's lecture the night before: *What would you think of doing some take?* I took. I took the chance—again.

"Yes, yes," I nodded. I heard some choking noises from Sylvia's direction. But I was crying now.

Harry was crying, too. "I mean, when you're eighteen, you can do whatever you want, but until then I thought you'd like to have some options.... We can fix up my spare room. You can have a real bed. You can have rainbows and unicorns—" (here I made a face) "or, or, or paint the walls black and be rebellious if you want." I got up and went around the table and sat in his lap and hugged him like I used to when I was little. He kissed my puffy hair.

"I'll go pack some things," I said.

"I'll go with you," Jeff said, following me up the stairs. A stony silence closed on the living room behind us.

8
A FAIRYTALE ENDING

“This is where you live?” Jeff made the sharp turn at the top of the narrow stairs and ducked into the attic room behind me.

“Not anymore, I guess,” I said, surveying the room. Dust motes twinkled in the stillness as the late spring sunlight streamed in through the small open window. Since I’d awakened three hours ago, the square of brightness had crawled like a slow spotlight down the length of my unmade bed and was now touching the stack of cardboard boxes. I pulled an old Samsonite out from behind them and dumped the contents—my old baby clothes—onto the bed.

We talked a little while I packed. Jeff hadn’t been over to the house since before Dad married Sylvia. “I remember the last time I was here,” he said.

“We were studying for something,” I recalled.

“French,” he said. “We were watching *The Red Balloon*, when the Hills came over for dinner. Debra and Donna were sort of fun back then.” We both smiled, remembering the Tic-Tac game.

“Yeah, things have changed a bit,” I said, trying to decide what to take, my senses sharp as I pawed through the wardrobe, realizing I was about to leave my home. I was keenly aware of my parents’ stuff in the boxes and trunks around me. The family photos. The old clothes and trinkets. The antique sewing machine. The lamps and chairs in the corner. The bentwood rocking chair with the broken caning. The hand-hooked rag rug and the patchwork quilt that had crossed a prairie with a grandmother.

"Maybe we could start watching French movies again at my house," he suggested.

"Entre Nous?" I flirted, glancing up at his dancing green eyes. Something passed between us.

"I'm such an idiot for not recognizing you last night," he said, smacking his head. "I'm so glad you tricked me."

I shrugged.

"Did you read all of these books?" Jeff was perusing the stacks of hardbacks and paperbacks on the shelves around the knee wall. He ran his hands along the Zs – I filed them alphabetically, sort of— *Zen and the Art of Motorcycle Maintenance, Zorba the Greek, Search for the Zipperump-a-Zoo.*

"Just up to under the window," I said. "I'm going to miss them all." Jeff picked up a dog-eared copy of *The Once and Future King*. "Can I borrow this?"

I smiled. "Of course." I looked down in my hands, which were holding *Goddesses in Everywoman*.

"What's that one?"

"It's great," I began, thinking of princesses, but I didn't get to finish. He reached out for it, but instead of taking the book, he grabbed my wrist.

"Hey, speaking of French," he said, pulling me closer, "we were interrupted last night." The book fell to the floor. My whole body tingled as I slid my hands up his shoulders and leaned in. When his lips touched mine, it was nothing like the big deal I'd always fantasized; it felt normal and natural and, well, quite simply, as delicious and as compelling as my first taste of ice cream. I laughed.

"What," he said.

I touched my mouth. "My stiff upper lip," I joked. "It's been that way for such a long time." He tenderly kissed it; neither of us could keep from smiling.

"You've probably been keeping a stiff lower lip, too." He moved his mouth.

"Might take some time to un-stiffen them both," I said. So we worked on that a little bit.

I said, "Can I ask you a question?"

He said, "Would you like to ask me another?"

I said, "Was it the shoes?"

"The shoes are pretty fabulous," he replied. "Even a dumb straight jock like me could see that."

"Jeff, you're not a—"

"Ashley—why did you ask?"

"I mean—" I blushed, embarrassed to ask what was really on my mind. I just blurted it out: "Do you really want to lick my toes?"

He laughed. "Can I?"

I pulled away, hiding my cheeks—red with pink swirls, I imagined! “We’ll have to work up to that.” I grabbed my backpack and took The Dress in my arms. Jeff lugged the big suitcase down the stairs, knocking walls, thumping a hollow goodbye.

Passing Donna’s room on the landing, we heard voices, and sobs. I knocked and twisted the knob. “Juicy” and “Pink” were spelled across the bodies on the bed. The sisters sat up and Debra said, “You can come in.”

“I wanted to say goodbye, you guys,” I said.

“Goodbye?”

“Harry asked me to come live with him,” I said.

“You can’t go!” Donna’s first impulse felt really nice. It could have gone the other way.

“Oh, my, God,” said Debra, her adorable little nose starting to wrinkle in judgment.

“He *is* my godfather,” I said, not wanting to elaborate.

“Can you fix the curtain before you go?” Donna asked, pointing to a tilted rod.

“Is Jeff still here?” Debra asked.

“I’m right here,” Jeff said, sticking his head in behind me. “Hi.”

The Girls jumped up to check their hair and then invited us properly in. Debra said, “We have something to ask you.”

“Ask away,” Jeff said.

“Okay, we know we’re not popular,” said Debra.

“And we know our mom meant well,” said Donna.

"But why? I mean, why not?" said Debra. "We're cheerleaders, we wear cute clothes, we have hot bods, we have all the latest stuff, we're friendly and outgoing."

"We try so hard," said Donna.

"Maybe you try *too* hard," said Jeff.

"Oh," they both said, surprised.

"I mean, remember that time you texted me your boobs? Why would you DO that?"

"Um," said Debra. "Because when you passed me in the hall you were totally glancing at them. I know that striped sweater made them look awesome."

"And they were, at the time, brand new," said Donna, gazing enviously at her sister's breasts. "She got them for her 18th birthday present."

"Yeah," said Debra. "And no one said anything. Just the usual jerks."

"I'm sorry," said Jeff, trying not to laugh. "I should have just gone and made a compliment. It was rude of me to peek out of the corner of my eye."

"Can you give us any advice?" Donna said. "I mean, in spite of our, our *everything*, we really have a hard time meeting the *right* people."

"Um, maybe," said Jeff, reaching for my hand, "we could double, I mean, triple date sometime. I have some friends, could introduce you...."

"That would be *awesome*," said Donna, her eyes sparking with excitement.

Debra eyed our hands, confused. “Are you two... together?”

“Yeah, Jeff, are you asking me on a date?” I squeezed his hand and he nodded.

“Then who was that girl last night who....?” Donna looked puzzled. Then Debra got it and she elbowed her sister. They looked at each other wide-eyed, then looked at us again, differently this time.

“Was it *you*?” Debra asked. I nodded.

“No! WAY!” Donna said. The two of them looked so conflicted, remembering how they treated me last night before they left, remembering their frustration when Jeff chose me, remembering the approval of the crowd and—the significance of the event dawned on them much quicker than it did me—realizing my newfound social status. Disdain, anger, and admiration flickered over their faces and finally they settled on a feeling. I was so incredibly glad it was wonder, and approval.

“Oh, my, God,” said Donna. “Our stepsister is the most popular girl in the school!” They hugged each other to celebrate this new victory. Their words sunk in and I started to wonder what Monday would be like. I would be rocketed into a new life—if the rest of the student body ever put two and two together—which they would if Jeff ever walked me to class and... Jeff nodded, pulled me closer, as if to reassure me that we could take it slowly.

And there would be my stepsisters. Who, even though my father was gone and we no longer had a legal relationship, would always be my special um, step-somethings. Suddenly it struck me the difference between the two of them and me: *they had only ever had Sylvia for a mom.*

"Do you have something I could write on?" I asked, suddenly wanting to cry. Donna reached for her empty diary, which she kept on a shelf above her bed. I flipped it open and jotted some notes down. "For later," I said, "when you don't know what to do."

Donna got up and grabbed something else from another cluttered shelf across the room. "Here. Before you go, Ashley. I want you to have this." She pulled down a six-inch glass Pegasus with a thick, graceful, arched neck, whose wings stretched forwards as if to gather speed, and whose muscled hindquarters were gathered as if she were about to explode free of the glass base.

"Thank you so much," I said, hugging her and crying for real. "You don't know what this means to me."

Her expression grew as clear as I'd ever seen it. "Actually, I do," she said.

"You can have my glass unicorn," I told her. "They lay their horns in the laps of virgins." Donna made a face to her sister like I was crazy. "And the pure of heart," I added. "Plus," I said, as Jeff and I turned to leave the room, "they can heal anything."

DATE 4-ever

Parting Advice for D & D...

If you open it, close it.

If you turn it on, turn it off.

If you break it, fix it or have it fixed.

If you borrow it, return it.

If you make a mess, clean it up.

If you use it, take care of it.

If you move it, put it back.

If it's not yours, ask first.

If you don't know how it works, learn.

If you feel like criticizing, suggest instead.

If you make a promise, keep it.

If you mess up, apologize.

If you don't want it, don't waste it.

and

If you don't mean it, don't say it.

Be Sweet,

Ashley

As we came down the last flight of stairs, we heard loud voices and stopped to make faces at each other. Down in the living room, Harry and Sylvia were continuing the argument they'd started from the dance floor.

Harry was talking about my dad. "He was such a loving person," he shouted. "You destroyed him, and then you moved on to his daughter, to crush her, too."

Sylvia spat, "You're just jealous I married him, aren't you?"

Harry sat down heavily. "I can't deny that."

"Hah!" Sylvia cried. Jeff and I looked at each other, eyes wide.

"You know I really loved him," Harry sighed. "I loved them both. They loved me, too."

Sylvia startled at his honesty, then attacked again. "How can you be so selfish, knowing what I've been through? How *dare* you say that to me?"

"How dare *I*?" Harry roared. "How dare *you*! You've tied Ashley down with all of your menial busywork. You've exhausted her spirit! You've *denied* her the *gorgeous* un*folding* that is the *right* of a girl in her teens!"

Sylvia denied everything. "What are you *talking* about? I love her like my own daughters," which of course made Harry snort.

He spelled it out like only a barrister-drag queen could, stabbing his finger in Sylvia's direction as if it could shoot magical fire: "You have stifled her will, abused her rights, made her your slave, and deprived her of her *much-needed* beauty sleep!" Sylvia sputtered nonsense syllables; Harry confronted her and spat, "You won't even look me in the eye!"

Suddenly Sylvia recovered and shot out, "What the *hell* were you doing at the prom last night anyway, all dragged up? I can't figure you out! Did you just come there to get in my face?"

Harry shook his head with pity. "You really don't get it, do you? I was there with Ashley."

Sylvia barked. "Hah, that's a laugh. She was here at home. Looking like a 'before' picture with her sweatpants and tennies. She had plenty to do."

She looked up to see Jeff and I standing on the stairs. She saw me holding The Dress and fell silent. Then it all came clear to her. Tears streamed down her face. Now it was her turn to sit down hard. She realized her defeat.

Harry spoke quietly as he stood up. "Well darling, things are going to change now. You're going to lose your house slave. You can kiss my big, hairy ass, and kiss your reign of terror good-bye! Let's go, Ashley."

Then I said the words I'd been longing to say. "Goodbye, Sylvia." Jeff held the door open. Harry slammed it emphatically after he went through, and took my things from me. He put them in the back seat of his convertible. The three of us looked at each other, not sure what to say next.

"My ass isn't really that hairy," Harry finally muttered.

"That's okay," I said. Jeff laughed. And then I said, "Thank you, Harry."

"Well, I guess you know everything now," Harry said, still sorting himself out. "I—"

"Thank you, Harry," said Jeff.

Harry looked at Jeff, as if for the first time. "Thank *you*," he said, wiping his hands on his slacks, still trying to compose himself. "Glad you were here." And then they regarded each other for some time. "So what was your plan," Harry asked, "when you showed up this morning?"

"I just wanted to see if Ashley wanted to hang out for a little bit. Maybe go for a drive." Harry glanced over at Jeff's little car, a brick red vintage Volvo sports coupe, handed down to him by his grandfather on his 16th birthday. He sighed.

"Okay," he said. "You kids do that. I'll take your stuff home, Ashley. It will give me time to cool off, and get things ready for you."

"Okay," I said, hardly believing how great this moment was.

"But one thing," Harry said, as if realizing all at once that a) he was now my parent, and b) I was about to get in a car with a boy. He said, a little too loud, "seat belts."

"Oh, of course," said Jeff, a total Boy Scout. "Always."

"Always," Harry emphasized. "Even when the car is parked. Understand me?" He shook his head, no doubt

remembering the scene from the parking lot last night, wondering what the heck he was doing, becoming the parent of a teenager.

Jeff shook his hand and smiled, "Yes, sir." Then he glanced at me and shrugged. We all laughed.

Jeff and I buckled up for safety—and temperance—while Harry drove away. Jeff pulled out into the street, but before we had gotten too far, he stopped.

"We forgot the shoes."

Awkward.

We crept back into the living room, hoping to grab them from the windowsill and go, but Sylvia was still sprawled where we had left her, staring into space. Light played over her fraying hair from the glass beads when we moved the shoes.

"Ashley," she said, looking up, "I'm sorry."

Startled, I turned to stare. I had never heard her say those words.

Her eyes went from liquid to solid in an instant, as the warm and cold parts of her personality collided. "If you walk through that door, I swear to God, you will never get an ounce of support from me again," she threatened. "You are leaving your HOME behind! How could you do that?" Behind me, Jeff snorted.

"I don't want to," I said quietly, "but Harry's right. I don't have to take care of you anymore. I'm tired of you yelling at me all the time. I'm tired of doing all the work and being called names. I deserve better than this. Harry appreciates me for who I am."

Sylva's eyes softened again, and she said, "I am just so angry right now I can't stand it. But Harry's right. You don't have to stay. You are winning, and I am losing the one thing I have left of your dad. Who I really loved."

She started crying again. Why hadn't she ever said this before? We had that in common. "Oh, Sylvia," I said, feeling tears come to my own eyes.

"Can you just do me one favor?" She asked in a voice that I hadn't heard for years. "Can you please help me clean this mess up? I just can't... I just don't know how I'll get through the day. With the girls and all. And then tomorrow..."

I looked at Jeff, who looked a little worried, and then looked at Sylvia sitting there, looking so desperate, and realized I could end this on my terms. The mess she was referring to was a nicely set buffet table—with mom's china—a few dirty dishes, and a pile of papers on the floor by her desk. I lifted my chin and said, "of course, Sylvia." Together, we stacked the plates up and put them back in the cabinet. She poured the punch down the drain and I folded the tablecloth—the way *I* wanted it folded. I put the punch bowl safely back in the attic, closed the curtain, made my bed, found the key, and locked the door behind me. Downstairs, Jeff helped me put the plastic slipcovers back on, and scooped up the piles of paper that had fallen from by the desk earlier.

"Ashley," Jeff called out, excited. "There's mail for you."

At that sound, Sylvia came rushing back into the living room officiously and said, "You know, maybe *I* should be the one to clean up my desk. You guys can go."

"It's a letter from Castleton," Jeff said. He handed it to me and I tore it open. I could not believe what I read.

"They accepted me," I squealed. And then when I got to the second page, I shouted, "And a scholarship!" I jumped up and down. This was the dream I had been waiting for. Jeff hugged me and twirled me around.

"I'm going there, too," he said. This was the dream I could never have hoped for.

Sylvia stuttered. "I-I was waiting for Debra and Donna's letters to come so I could give them to you all at the same time." Her voice was unsure.

"Goodbye, Sylvia," I said for the last time. "Take care." Then I took that one big step out the front door.

Into my own magnificent life.

April 1st

Dear Ms. Saint Helens,

As you probably know already, you have been accepted to Castleton College for the fall semester of this year! It is with great delight we welcome you to our learning community! Your matriculating class is the highest-achieving ever, and between your exemplary commitment to learning, your financial need, and your sparkling entrance essays, you have been awarded the Merlin Scholarship for full tuition, plus the Perrault Stipend for room and board! (!!!!) Congratulations, my dear!

Please contact us before midnight on May 15th with your decision to accept this prestigious award! Your future awaits!

Enthusiastically Yours,

Abby Dean

Abigal Dean
Dean of Admissions
Castleton College
Black Forest, MW 44883

Bonus Material

FOR THE NEW EDITION

ENDNOTES & ESSAYS

by Ashley St. Helens and her beloved professor of Mythology & Folklore, Dr. Mädchen März

---

i. THE THIRD GENDER IN MYTH AND FOLKLORE

By Mädchen März, Ph.D.

Mythology, history, folklore and literature bring us hundreds, perhaps thousands of interesting examples of the "third gender," which includes ambiguously sexual or transgender people in all cultures who walk between being a man and a woman. This type of person does not fit into roles defined by gender, althouhg some societies try to force them to. In some cultures and myths, these individuals are revered, while in others they are demonized. In some, like ours, it's both; comedians (such as Ricky Gervais) and cartoon characters (such as Bugs Bunny) delight with their cross-dressing habits, while young people are beaten and killed even on rumors that they're gay. The value of these unique beings (who are genetically defined by science) is that they can provide insight that the community needs.

"Clothing makes the man," so the saying goes.

It makes the man (or the woman) into anything s/he wants!

A short list of well-known cross-dressing characters includes Achilles, Athena, and Aphrodite's worshippers, Thor, Odin, Loki and Krishna; Mulan, Joan of Arc, and George Sand; Don Juan, Huckleberry Finn, and Eowyn; many characters in Shakespeare and Monty Python; Victor/Victoria, Madamme Butterfly, Frank N. Furter, and Mrs. Doubtfire. Dame Edna, Divine and RuPaul are men who are celebrated for dressing like and acting

Mythology, history, folklore and literature bring us hundreds, perhaps thousands of interesting examples of the "third gender," which includes ambiguously sexual or transgender people in all cultures who walk the line between being a man and a woman. This type of person does not fit into roles defined by gender, although some societies try to force them to. In some cultures and myths, these individuals are revered; in others they are demonized. In our society, it's both—comedians (such as Ricky Gervais) and cartoon characters (such as Bugs Bunny) delight with their cross-dressing habits, while young people are still beaten and killed by closed-minded thugs even on rumors that they're gay. The value of these unique beings (who are genetically defined by science) is that they can provide insight that the community needs, and benefit society as a whole by living as their authentic selves.

A short list of well-known cross-dressing characters includes Achilles, Athena, and Aphrodite's worshippers; Thor, Odin, Loki and Krishna; Mulan, Joan of Arc, and George Sand; Don Juan, Huckleberry Finn, and Eowyn; many characters in Shakespeare and Monty Python; Victor/Victoria, Madamme Butterfly, Frank N. Furter, and Mrs. Doubtfire. Dame Edna, Divine and RuPaul are men who are celebrated for dressing like and acting like outrageous women.

If you've never cross-dressed for Halloween or another costume party, I highly recommend it. Even I enjoy cross-dressing from time to time. And then cross-dressing back.

March, Mädchen, Ph.D., Ed.D., Bf.D. "The Third Gender in Myth and Folklore." *Teen Princess Magazine* vol. 33 (1987)

reprinted with permission

ii. BOOKS UNDER ASHLEY'S BED

The book that the line on p. 12 is from is *Wise Child* by Monica Furlong, a wonderful book about white witches. Other books under Ashley's bed include classic novels like Kafka's *Metamorphosis*, Tolstoy's *War and Peace*, *Zen and the Art of Motorcycle Maintenance* by Robert Pirsig, *Zorba the Greek* by Nikos Kazantsakis and *The Once and Future King* by T.H. White; scores of philosophy and psychology books like the *Goddesses in Everywoman* by Jean Shinoda Bolen she waves around, and *On the Wings of Self-Esteem*; plus boxes of childhood favorites like *Professor Wormbog and the Search for the Zipperump-a-Zoo* by Mercer Mayer, everything by Dr. Seuss; and all her mom's cookbooks. Follow the author on GoodReads for a longer list of titles, since they've read a lot of the same boks. Oh, and if you ever meet a high school student who has read all the books Ashley has, they might be a fictional character. Pinch them to be sure, then ask them what they've read lately!

iii. THE GIRDLE: POWER SYMBOL OR FAT FIGHTER?

By Ashley St. Helens

Ashley wrote this essay in Dr. März's *Intro to Folklore* class, where she met her friends Nevada LeBlanc and Linda Loveland. Over the next few years, both of them also found themselves living in "fairytale realities." It was the most peculiar thing, but when Dr. März heard about the contest they were glad to be able to tell their stories.

Mythology 101 February 18, 2001

The Girdle: Power Symbol or Fat Fighter?

by Ashley St. Helens

A+

To "gird" means to encircle, surround, or to bind, also to prepare. A girdle does just that to the body, compressing the hips, thighs, and abdomen.

To my generation, a girdle is a symbol of old-fashioned restriction, repression, and propriety that one associates with unfit, self-loathing older women, although the body shapers that young women rely on to mask figure flaws are essentially no different. However, my research on girdles in mythology has shown me that girdles are rich with meaning and power.

In ancient Egyptian, Greek, and Minoan cultures, plus many more I am sure, the girdle was a practical part of a person's clothing of either sex, especially when fashions were long and draped or short and loose. Girdle was a word used for simple leather belts, fancy embroidered or beaded tapestries tied at the waist, or strong and jewel-encrusted metal casings for the waist and hips. Sometimes in mythological readings, girdles also bind breasts, like a corset.

The power of the girdle comes, I believe, from the place on the body which it holds; there is a lot going on between the waist and thighs. Our rear ends and thighs are made of the muscles that move us; our abdomens contain digestive organs essential to our health, and of course a woman's reproductive organs reside within her abdomen, as well. One version of the metal girdle became the locked chastity belt, or "girdle of purity." In the middle ages, the idea of this device made enough of an impact on textile fashion that girdles became a symbol of virginity and virtue, and prostitutes (in France, at least,) were not allowed to wear them. What we wear around our privates also seems to be important enough to have taken its place in mythology.

Ishtar, the Egyptian goddess of fertility, love, sex, and (I don't really get this,) war, had a fertility girdle. Aphrodite's magical girdle had the power to inspire the passion of desire, and she would loan it to other goddesses to help them with their love-troubles. Supposedly it was made of gold filigree, crafted lovingly by Hephaestus, her husband. Weathermen refer to a pink glow on the horizon right before sunrise or after sunset as "The Belt of Venus." Hercules actually killed Hippolyte to get her girdle as his ninth labor, even though she would have given it to him freely.

The great warriors of Homer wore girdles to protect them from arrows, Odysseus, and Sir Gawain many futures later, both accept green girdles from women (Calypso and Lady Bercilak, respectively). Thor, the Norse god of thunder, wears a girdle of might that even has a name: Megingjarpar. St. George borrows a girdle from a princess to help tame a dragon. Metaphorical girdles such as Tolkien's girdle of Melian—a protective enchantment around an elf kingdom—and the girdle of righteousness found both in the Bible and World of Warcraft, also abound in mythology.

Do mortals feel this magic when they wear girdles? Their popularity attests to this idea. When girdles became undergarments in the 20th century, the advertisements in which we see them seem to engender the wearer with a Venus-like aura of love, desire, beauty, magnetism and charm. Cross-dressing males glorify girdles for their erotic powers as much as women do. Today's girdles are standard armor in war as well, if only in the war against fat. Girdles of today squeeze fat in to hide or redistribute it, or support the body for exercise, as in compression shorts or football girdles that keep thigh pads in place for "battle."

What is next for the girdle? In the 1950s, no woman would be without her modern rubberized elastic girdle with hook-and-eye technology, any more than a woman of the 1850s would be without her boned and busked corsets. Both were used to hold stockings up, but panty hose that combined panties and hose held themselves up with the miracle fabric of nylon, made girdles and corsets obsolete, as well as the rigid, controlled feminine waist. Today's space-age fabrics such as lycra, spandex, and neoprene have helped the girdle evolve into shapewear foundation garments as well as wetsuits, bathing suits, and exercise clothing. Companies like Speedo, Nancy Ganz, Under Armour and Spanx reveal their own modern mythologies to consumers through commercials.

iv. STEP-PING ON MY TOES

Rivalry of Blended Families in Grimm's Universe and Pop Culture

by Mädchen März, Ph.D.

EXPLORING MYTH AND MYSTERIES

"Step-ping" On My Toes

Rivalry of Blended Families in Grimm's Universe and Pop Culture

MADCHEN MARCH, PH.D.

Mythology is full of stepfamilies. Consider Zeus himself, who bore children willy-nilly with titans (Leto was the mother of Apollo and Artemis;), goddesses (his wife Hera was the mother of Ares), mortals (Alcmene was the mother of Hercules). Norse, Hindu, and Chinese mythologies contain plenty of stories about blended families that turn out for better or worse. Fairytales and folklore are full of step-children, from Cinderella to Snow White to vulnerable Hansel and Gretel. Perhaps this is because stepfamilies have always been a part of life. Even today, about half of the 60 million children under the age of thirteen in the U.S. are living with one biological parent and one non-biological adult.

A mythopoetic look at stepfamilies is useful for those who are in one. For just as racism and sexism are clear and systematic habits of institutional discrimination, so is the reality of parental favoritism in families, across all generations and cultures, with few enlightened exceptions. Our understanding of this intimate social dynamic can be deepened by examining its intricacies through the lens of fairy tales and folklore, in particular by focusing on the phenomenon of stepfamilies, which are prevalent in this type of literature.

Common problems described by stepchildren include feeling unwanted by a stepparent; feeling alienated within the new family; being torn by tension. The feeling of being loved and valued is related to self-esteem, and because of the difficulty in connecting with adults in a deep and emotionally meaningful way, it can be difficult for children in stepfamilies to maintain theirs. Love and value must be overt.

Cinderella's stepfamily has inspired studies on The Cinderella Effect, which documents abuse by step-parents. There is plenty of evidence that supports this phenomenon finding that when abusive parents have both step and genetic children, they generally spare their genetic children. In such families, stepchildren were exclusively targeted 9 out of 10 times in one study and in 19 of 22 in another. In addition to abusing children at higher rates, stepparents display fewer positive behaviors than genetic parents. They don't take stepchildren to the doctor as often, play with them less, pay less for their education, and so forth. Since stepchildren are often the oldest ones in the family, they are more often discriminated against in blended families, whereas in families that are not blended the youngest tend to be most frequent victims.

However, such discrimination is rarely evident in modern mythology, which loves stepfamilies with

(This article by Professor März provided Ashley with insight into both the Cinderella folktale and her own family.)

Mythology is full of stepfamilies. Consider Zeus himself, who bore children willy-nilly with titans (Leto was the mother of Apollo and Artemis;), goddesses (his wife Hera was the mother of Ares), mortals (Alcmene was the mother of Hercules). Norse, Hindu, and Chinese mythologies contain plenty of stories about blended families that turn out for better or worse. Fairytales and folklore are full of step-children, from Cinderella to Snow White to vulnerable Hansel and Gretel. Perhaps this is because stepfamilies have always been a part of life. Even today, about half of the 60 million children under the age of thirteen in the U.S. are living with one biological parent and one non-biological adult.

A mythopoetic look at stepfamilies is useful for those who are in one. For just as racism and sexism are clear and systematic habits of institutional discrimination, so is the reality of parental favoritism in families, across all generations and cultures, with few enlightened exceptions. Our understanding of this intimate social dynamic can be deepened by examining its intricacies through the lens of fairy tales and folklore, in particular by focusing on the phenomenon of stepfamilies, which are prevalent in this type of literature.

Common problems described by stepchildren include feeling unwanted by a stepparent; feeling alienated within the new family; being torn by tension. The feeling of being loved and valued is related to self-esteem, and because of the difficulty in connecting with adults in a deep and emotionally meaningful way, it can be difficult for children in stepfamilies to maintain theirs. Love and value must be overt.

Cinderella's stepfamily has inspired studies on The Cinderella Effect, which documents abuse by step-parents. There is plenty of evidence that supports this phenomenon finding that when abusive parents have both stepchildren and biological children, they generally spare their genetic heirs. In such families, stepchildren were exclusively targeted 9 out of 10 times in one study and in 19 of 22 in another. In addition to abusing children at higher rates, stepparents display fewer positive behaviors than genetic parents. They don't take stepchildren to the doctor as often, play with them less, pay less for their education, and so forth. Since stepchildren are often the oldest ones in the family, they are more often discriminated against in blended families, whereas in families that are not blended the youngest tend to be most frequent victims.

However, such discrimination is rarely evident in modern mythology, which loves stepfamilies with funny problems. *The Brady Bunch* was a blended family without any unresolved anger, feelings of loss and sadness, or even mention of the other, non-present parents—an unrealistic and unhelpful mirror for viewers with similar situations. *Modern Family* brings out the comedy inherent in family differences, but again, it is hard to really show families dealing with depression, guilt, and grief in a funny way.

The key to a happily blended family is parents who are conscious of the tendency for discrimination, and who can "be the grownups" in situations where children are grieving. When an adult marries into a broken family, they must allow the children to express their negative feelings, and respond with love and understanding, if the prognosis for a true fairytale ending is to be achieved.

March, Mädchen, Ph.D., Ed.D., Bf.D. "Stepping On My Toes: Rivalry of Blended Families in Grimm's Universe and Pop Culture." *The Facts of Mythology Magazine* 1099.1 (2010) ISSN: 5555-5555

MUSICAL SONG LYRICS!

"THE BIG BITCH"

ASHLEY: From the minute I wake up until I go to bed at night,
[sings] I have to do what they say or it turns into a fight.
It's not like I don't want to help;
they're just so full of spite.
Nothing's good enough for them!
I just can't do it right!
HARRY: *[speaks]* Look at you go! Let it all out!
ASHLEY: *[sings - through clenched teeth]*
Nag, nag, rag, rag, bitch, bitch, bitch!
[They both laugh.]
The only peace I find is when I'm way out of their sight.
HARRY: *[speaks]* So what else?
ASHLEY: *[sings]* Her expectations are too low.
Her standards are too high.
SYLVIA: You're folding all the towels wrong!
ASHLEY: It makes me want to cry.
DEBRA: Ashley, that's the wrong soap!
ASHLEY: —harps her snoopy little spy.
All these picayune details—why should I even try?
Nag, nag, rag, rag, bitch, bitch, bitch bitch bitch...
DONNA: Ashley, feed my GigaPet! I don't want him to die!
HARRY: *[speaks]* Okay. Deep breath. Let it all out.
ASHLEY: *[a ragged sigh.]*
[sings] They're slobs! I pick up everything!
Their keys and underwear!
They make me draw their bubble baths.
They make me brush their hair.
They make me sweep the closet floors,
and vacuum every stair.
I steam the carpets, make the coffee, purify the air!
ALL 4: *[singing-pantomiming chaos]*
Nag, nag, nag, rag, rag, rag,
bitch, bitch, bitch, bitch, bitch, bitch!
Bitch! Bitch! Bitch! Bitch! Bitch! Bitch!
ASHLEY: *[angrily]* Bitch! Bitch! Bitch!
[Sylvia, Donna and Debra exit hurriedly]
HARRY: Doesn't that...
ASHLEY: *[shouts]* Bitch!

HARRY: Doesn't that...
ASHLEY: Bitch...*[tentatively]*...es...
HARRY: *[Laughs, then speaks]* Now you're talking!
Doesn't that feel good?
ASHLEY: *[sings, sweetly, brightly]*
But there's one thing they can't make me do.
HARRY: And what's that, honey?
ASHLEY: CARE! *[sigh of release]*
HARRY: Oh, but you should!
[cackles] Just imagine...
[sings] They'll be eating cold, dry cereal—no more filet mignon!
ASHLEY: They'll have to add new coping skills to their old lexicons!
HARRY: They must break their co-dependencies
if they're to carry on,
ASHLEY: And learn to clean a litterbox and water their own lawn!
HARRY: Can't you see that bitch, bitch, bitch
Wearing stained and stinky cashmere sweaters when you're gone?
ASHLEY: *[cackles, then catches herself]*
[speaks] Oh Harry, I may feel mad but I don't want to be mean.
HARRY: Oh Ashley, you are so sweet! How *do* you keep yourself going?
[on this last verse, Debra, Donna and Sylvia waltz through grabbing things, leaving things, creating disorder with every move.]
ASHLEY: Just knowing that sometime—and soon—
[sings] My tenure's gonna end.
Someday my ship—my scholarship—
Will sail around the bend.
One day I'll escape this life, so all the time I spend
In solitude, my nose in books, makes it less pretend.
Rag rag, nag nag, bitch bitch helps.
They say that suffering builds character!
HARRY: *[speaks]* Well, you've certainly got character....
ASHLEY: *[speaks]* God, it's good to have a friend!

"IF THE SHOE FITS"

HARRY: You know, girl, a rose may be a rose may be a rose, but:

Anyone who says a shoe's a shoe is just a shoe eschews
the wisdom of the new, the few,
the women who know through and through

that whatever you do you're on a path,
be it to town or Timbuktu,
so blue, ecru, or any hue,
your shoes give you direction that is true.

ASHLEY: — I guess they do.

[Harry leads Ashley on a tour among the racks and stacks of shoes. Ashley draws it all in — she is a good student, but a little distracted by all there is to look at.]

HARRY: Footwear is important!
But you're never fully dressed without a smile—
so it's essential that your tootsies
honestly reflect your style,
If the shoe fits, and it's comfy, disregard the fashion file!
or walk a mile in someone else's moccasins
once in a while—

ASHLEY: — Ah yes. Be versatile.

[Harry reaches for shoes on racks, from above, and in bins to illustrate his points.]

HARRY: When you accessorize
the hemisphere beneath your thighs,
remember there's a purpose for every variety of shoe
(if you are wise)!
Wear fuzzy slippers to keep warm,
and steel-toed Docs to vandalize;
Flip-flops for the beach;
and for sports, Air Jordans help you to fantasize!
(and, my dear, they come in your size....)

ASHLEY: *[mutters]* Yeah, the only thing that comes in my size!

HARRY: Honey, you need to VISUALIZE!
[Harry picks up shoe after shoe from the shelf.]
Army boots with a parachute!
Dock shoes with a sailor suit!
Galoshes with a bumbershoot.
Mary Janes—AREN'T THEY CUTE!?
[Ashley nods, agreeably, and shrugs. She's starting to understand.]
Chucks, Vans, Sketchers, Keds—
Tennies go with casual threads.
Platform sneakers will turn heads!
Or wear penny loafers instead?
[Ashley is starting to understand.]

ASHLEY: Huaraches con un sombrero; Zoris with kimono;
Cowboy boots with a pointy toe—

BOTH: —are perfect for a doe-si-do!

[Harry gestures at a rack of back-less shoes.]

HARRY: Thongs and clogs and mules all rock—and stay on fine if you keep to a walk.
Birkenstocks that your cool friends mock—
ASHLEY: *[defensively]*—are very comfy worn with socks!
HARRY: *[pleading]*—Whatever you do, don't wear Crocs!
[As Harry approaches the high-heeled shoes, other shoppers become the chorus.]
H & CHORUS: But if you want to cause a scandal...*(Ooh, aah)*
Espadrilles can't hold a candle... *[Sigh, moan!]*
to a strappy, sassy, sexy sandal...
[A crazed shopper reaches up and grabs the hottest shoe from Harry.]
Manolos are too hot to handle!
[Harry points at a mannequin that subtly swings its hips to the rhythm.]
HARRY: Let me now enumerate the virtues of the evening shoe!
A stacked heel or stiletto elevates your view and helps legs grow six inches longer, leaner, luscious, curvy, hips a swingin' slow—men want to glorify your charms, and if you let them, lick your toes.
[Ashley gasps. The chorus gasps, too. But they gasp rapturously; she is quite grossed out by the idea.]
ASHLEY: Eew! Lick my toes!?
HARRY & CHORUS: Yes. Lick. Your. Toes.
[The chorus dances behind Harry as he rapturizes about shoes, sometimes kicking ("magnificent"), sometimes hobbling ("pain," "agony"). Meanwhile, Ashley shops to no avail—until ("marvelous shoes") she sees a pair of Lucite heels—pure and simple like her—but a little tacky for Harry's tastes. He makes a face ("agony"), but to Ashley nods encouragingly.]

Ah, shoes! Dramatic shoes! Ah, shoes! The power, the pleasure, of glorious shoes! Shoes! Magnificent shoes! Ah, shoes! The pleasure—and pain—of glorious shoes. Shoes! Luxurious shoes! Ah, shoes! The power, the pleasure of glorious shoes! Shoes! Marvelous shoes! The ecstasy—and agony—of glorious shoes!
[The chorus gathers around Harry and Ashley for this magical moment. Harry holds the elegant shoe up to catch the light, then kneels down to fit them on Ashley's feet.]

HARRY: Feel the magic all around us,
[speaks] Stand up confident and feel your power!
You're the woman of the hour;
Now or never it's your time

To let your love shine
(like your face you scoured in the shower)
Radiant as a flower.
NOW.
Don't forget the source of all your power!
Mother Earth.
Nature's Gifts.
Draw it in, girl, from the *souls* of your feet!

Write to the author for musical scores and instructions on how to share your performance with the Fairytale Reality Project!

THE FAIRYTALE REALITY PROJECT

Mirror Imag(in)e

Vain people suck.

Enchantment isn't everything...

THE Number THE Beast

ACKNOWLEDGMENTS

The influences on and contributions to this story have been multiple and myriad. A few pertinent characters to whom I am especially grateful are:

Daddy, who made me believe I deserved love. **Pablo**, my first-grade honeybunch, and all my sweethearts and handsome princes up through The One, a.k.a. **Dave**.

Damian for the screenplay; **Louise** for the eagle eyes; **Felix** for his surprise. My biggest fams.

Mary, who taught me about folding towels—(but in a *nice* way!)

David for that unwritten opera, which inspired me to keep going...

Michael, for writing that first amazing song—and all that flowed after that.

Leah, my muse of shoes and patroness, **Alexa** the Snow White to my Cinderella, Rhonda of the pretty feet, **Laurie** and my classmates in her School of Charm, where I learned the art of high d.r.a.g. (*dr*essing *a*s *g*irl) —and all the **Decobelles**, who danced the original kick-line in my mind.

Stephen, for coaching me on Harry's law career—and for dancing like a fool with me.

Frank Furter, who made us all wish we had had the balls to be that outrageous, and

Mom, who raised me not to be a princess but let me dream of being a queen.

There are so many others who have helped support the creation of this book and the musical, I can't name you all! But I am deeply and renewably grateful for everyone who donated to the fundraiser, read or sang a role, laughed out loud, gave me shoe trinkets, shared their stories, or lifted this tale up in any way. May your footwear never chafe.

And of course I owe a shout-out to the Brothers Grimm and Disney and all the whisperers of the Cinderella myth since forever!

—Kristen Caven

ABOUT THE AUTHOR

Kristen Caven grew up in a dysfunctional stepfamily, secretly reading lots of books to help maintain her cheerful childhood spirit. In college she learned to waltz and eventually graduated with a degree called *Myth and The Western Mind.* She was never into princesses but the world seemed obsessed with them. Over the next few years she began writing stories. As cartoons. And screenplays. And operas. In bed. One day her husband suggested that the shoes under her bed were the source of all her power. She woke up laughing a few nights later from a dream about a Cinderella with big feet.

Today Kristen is the author of many books and plays, and nourishes herself and others with her creativity and wisdom. She takes care of her community but aspires to be an international woman of mystery.

Her main website is www.kristencaven.com.

THE PHENOMENON

SHOE SALONS

Here's how to have a great party, based on this book: Invite your friends over, wearing a pair of shoes with a story behind them. Read the part where Harry discusses "shoe philosophy." Laugh, cry, and discuss... then take turns telling stories about where those shoes have taken everyone!

SHOE N' TELL

The Souls of Her Feet Facebook page hosts a Facebook group called *Shoe n' Tell!* —where members share pictures and tell stories about shoes, and their journeys.

Email: patchworkprincessproject@gmail.com

Page: www.facebook.com/The-Souls-of-Her-Feet

Group: www.facebook.com/groups/ShoeAndTell/

THE ORIGIN

Before she created Ashley St. Helens and *The Souls of Her Feet*, the author had a funny and prescient dream about being Cinderella. She recorded it faithfully as a cartoon narrative called *Not Exactly A Fairytale (Maybe a Dream Come True)*, which featured a swordfight with a doctor and Freudian Slippers. It's published in *The Reason She Left and*

Other Stories, available at www.kristencaven.com and in the usual places online.

Later, when Kristen was asked to write an opera libretto, she created *Shoes, a Mirror, and a Big Pink Rose,* a story of three young women with fairytale problems. Over the years it evolved into three musicals: *The Souls of Her Feet, Mirror Imag(in)e,* and *The Number the Beast.* This book was written while waiting for the music to be born.

THE OTHER EDITION

The original iBooks version of *The Souls of Her Feet (a musical cinderella)* includes an email subplot about the creators of the musical, plus audio, video, and graphic clips...check it out!

THE MUSICAL

The story is a bit different, but you can learn more about the musical at:

Website: www.thesoulsofherfeet.com

Twitter: @shoesmirrorrose

Facebook: Shoes, a Mirror, and a Big, Pink Rose

www.ingramcontent.com/pod-product-compliance
Lightning Source LLC
Chambersburg PA
CBHW070459170726
48291CB00008B/2570

9781950282494